the Peach Groves

Barbara Hanrahan

University of Queensland Press

c.3

By the same author

The Scent of Eucalyptus
Sea-Green
The Albatross Muff
Where the Queens all Strayed

Published by University of Queensland Press, St Lucia,
Queensland, 1979

Typeset by Press Etching Pty. Ltd., Brisbane.
Printed and bound by Southwood Press Pty. Ltd., Sydney.

Published with the assistance of the Literature Board of the
Australia Council.

National Library of Australia
Cataloguing in Publication data
Hanrahan, Barbara.
 The peach groves.

 ISBN 0 7022 1458 2
 ISBN 0 7022 1459 0 Paperback

 I. Title.

A823'.3

The author gratefully acknowledges the assistance of the
Literature Board of the Australia Council

To Jo Steele

You know, if the truth were known I have a perfect passion for the island where I was born. Well, in the early morning there I always remember feeling that this little island has dipped back into the dark blue sea during the night only to rise again at gleam of day, all hung with bright spangles and glittering drops . . . And just as on those mornings white milky mists rise and uncover some beauty, then smother it again and then again disclose it, I tried to lift that mist from my people and let them be seen and then to hide them again . . .

Katherine Mansfield to Dorothy Brett
11 October 1917

PART ONE

Glenelg; Epsom

The exotic New Zealand of which the
child Ida dreams in 1884 disappoints
when she and her mother and sister go
to visit; the genteel stuffing of colo-
nial respectability gradually pulls a-
part exposing coarse layers of violence
and illicit passion.

1

"There is a pattern," Blanche Dean was apt to sigh tiresomely, often. "God is good," she would say. "All is for the best."

It was easy to mouth the safe words close to home. She said them most frequently when she stood at the drawing-room window, gazing out past the laurels to the street that meant a less select world.

A soft smile pinched her lips as her hand caressed silk damask curtain. She fingered the Maltese cross that she habitually wore at her throat — ruby-studded, in the nicest taste — and her eyes watered a little at her luck. Dreamily, she smoothed her fingers over the swell of bosom that the crucifix countered. The bronze taffeta was new, and gave off a lovely rustle. So safe. And Blanche stroked her breasts and went on thanking God and banished last night's picture of George straining forward, the sickly smile of passion blurring the fact that he was a member of the Adelaide upper ten. Dear George.

His eyes might bulge and his laugh suggest a dangerous attack of the hiccups, but he was the lawyer of class who'd provided it all — taffeta and rubies, fashionable watering-place villa . . . the spaniel Boson nuzzling her feet, the ponies Dandie and Dash in the stables. It was George who'd transformed Betsy Jones of Liverpool, England to Blanche Dean of Glenelg, South Australia. All she had to do to live up to the "Blanche" was to remember her vowels and simper when conversation lapsed. George didn't merely mean nighttime fumbling and the fear that she had mixed her dates. There was membership of the House of Assembly and a spell as mayor; there were the little girls, ushered in by Nurse, all ringlets and eyelet embroidery . . . dear Maud running forward to kiss Mama's cheek, careful not to smudge her complexion; not quite so dear Ida following suit.

It was easy: God was good. The pattern stretched obligingly onward. "Chin up, little sister," commanded Harry when he sailed to New Zealand, and she had heeded him.

Harry had prospered, too. Adelaide hadn't suited, but Auckland proved just the right thing. The troublesome "Jones" was dealt with by treating it to the rank of Major. Which led on to marriage with Cissie, whose money did wonders, as well. The separation wasn't so bad. Each week, all the years, Harry's letter had come. Cissie sounded a dud.

And then Postie brought a letter that was special. Because of it, Mama and Papa went into the drawing-room and banged the door, and Mama's voice was raised so high that she seemed in a rage. This wasn't an unusual occurrence, Papa's pet name for Mama being Pepper-box; but then Ida heard Papa's voice, too. He was out of temper, also.

So Ida eavesdropped, and it was worth it: she told the doll, Queechy, first. Queechy proved a satisfactory listener. At Ida's news her porcelain cheeks flushed pinker, her eyes opened wide. Maud's face stayed pale when Ida went on to tell her. She shook her head disapprovingly, concentrating on the error of listening at doors. New Zealand stopped being magic.

You might have known, Queechy breathed silently, sympathetically. Ida felt better and the magic returned.

Maud was sensible and spoilt things. She was as pretty as Mama, but in her case all that peaches and cream and abundance of silvery hair — those dimples and forget-me-not eyes — were wasted. Miss Maud was as virtuous as an angel, said Nurse, and Ida sniggered with jealousy, and knew that if she'd resembled Mama instead of taking after the Deans (pleasant enough, but oh — those pudgy fingers and roly-poly bodies, that ginger hair) she'd have contrived to live a perfect life, perhaps thrillingly immured in a tower or, on a more outdoor level, mixed up with highwaymen or maybe the ghost of Ned Kelly.

Maud was beautiful but good. On their Sunday walks down the narrow unmarked lanes that wound between other people's villas to the Esplanade and the lighthouse at the end of the jetty, she kept her eyes fixed prudently ahead. It was always Ida who saw the crocodile of afflicteds from the Home for Incurables, the sinister face with its unsightly blemish. Maud kept close to Nurse and took care not to tread in a dog's mess. She smiled gently at the day, even when the sun had gone in. She looked as if she liked wearing the gloves and stays that guaranteed her to be an offspring of class. On Sundays, Ida trailed behind disconsolate. Life was boring. Once, where they walked, there had been gum-trees and banksia roses, and the sky was mazed with parakeets. Blackfellows ran about naked; the old gods cared enough to menace. But the pioneers had come and, with them, Glenelg. Reed huts were replaced by a select marine retreat. The governor's summer residence arose; Mr McDonald imported three omnibuses from Glasgow (*The Thistle*, *The Shamrock* and *The Rose* were painted in assorted Scottish tartans for the run to the city). Then came a railway and the Terminus Hotel. And greasy poles and Aunt Sallies in season, and the Church of Christ. Glenelg, 1884: Maud and Ida walked out over the sea with Nursie and didn't bother to wonder at progress.

But New Zealand, where Uncle Harry lived, was different. The geographical reader mentioned volcanic forces and geysers, glaciers and snow-capped peaks. There were creeping plants with rope-like stems and trees two hundred feet high. And the kiwi, a bird lacking wings and tail; the White and Pink Terraces, which some nominated the eighth wonder of the world.

New Zealand was Ida's dreamland. Though sometimes she wondered. For the reader made even Australia sound interesting: twenty-five times the size of Great Britain, containing every kind of land, from barren desert to richest soil. And Adelaide was known as Queen City of the South, and its gardens were among the loveliest in the world. In summer in Adelaide, the book published in London assured, flowers of the rarest kind flourished in all their beauty, the air was filled with perfume, there were shady walks of thick evergreens. But last summer in the garden at Glenelg, the annuals had wilted and the lawns resembled coconut matting . . . And, from his letters, Uncle Harry's life didn't seem so foreign to theirs.

But Queechy's glass eyes were reassuring. The wise look was on her face, and Ida felt comforted. It didn't matter that Maud wasn't impressed. She had heard Mama read the letter, and Aunt Cissie was sick, and Uncle Harry wanted them to come. Then Papa's voice had claimed a turn, and then they were talking together. Papa said it was impossible; that they should never be parted. Mama replied that it was her duty to the brother she loved. She said that it wouldn't be for long; that the chicks would find the visit educational.

Their voices went on, but Ida stopped listening. Mama would win. She always did.

That night in bed she thought about giant trees and Uncle. Years and years ago, strong hands had hovered above her head and by-passed Maud to swing her high in the air. "That's my girl," Uncle had cried, and she crowed with joy as he crushed her against his jacket. Though he smelled of cigars, Uncle might have been a character from *Pilgrim's Progress*. He was more like an angel than a man.

Uncle Harry was laughing and kind. He was an

adventurer who lived up north. He dug in the ground — not for gold, but gum. Uncle lived on a gum-field, and you'd think there'd be trees, but he said No, hardly any. They'd all been cut down; there were only the pieces of gum to prove they'd been there. Ida thought it must be like digging for marbles or eggs . . . Some people up north lived in tents, but Uncle had a hut. Uncle could cook damper; he knew gum-diggers who were really earls in disguise.

Ida loved remembering about Uncle, but Maud could ruin even that. She said Ida was making the stories up; that her memories were fibs. The part about the gum-field and the hut might be true, but that was because Mama had told her. "You were only a baby when he came," said Maud. "If I can't remember him coming, how can you?"

Uncle had brought Ida and Maud necklaces of speckled seeds as a present. Maud had lost her necklace, but Ida's was safe in the velvet box beside her corals. That was proof, if you needed it, that he'd really come. And in Mama's jewel box was the kauri-gum heart. Uncle had carved it for her specially, and sometimes Mama wore it on a ribbon round her neck.

So Ida kept on thinking of Uncle Harry — of how kind he was, how handsome. She even felt glad that Maud couldn't recall him. Because she couldn't, he seemed solely related to Ida.

Papa was kind, too, but he kept his distance. He didn't laugh much. His hands were soft and pink; they didn't come out to touch you like Uncle Harry's tanned ones. Uncle laughed a lot and was jolly. The day he took her to the races, Mama laughed too, and wore violets pinned to her collar. They were a striking pair, Mama and Uncle — both tall, though she was the Snow Queen, silver and white, while he had black hair and the sun-tan.

Race day was one of Ida's favourite rememberings. She could see the two of them as plain as anything — Mama and Uncle Harry, with the great crowd milling about them: the ladies all plumes and flowers, the gentlemen with embroidered waistcoats. There was a band playing somewhere in the distance, and lots of long-leg horses, silky and shimmering, with jockeys like monkeys crouched to their backs. Ida remembered so well, she even saw herself there, too, jumping up and down as the horse Uncle bet on won. Everyone was cheering — the pretty plumed ladies and the elegant gentlemen — as Wapiti streaked past the judges' box.

After he married Aunt Cissie, Uncle Harry had race-horses of his own. Each time Mama read out one of his letters, and it mentioned Nelson or Wapiti's form, Papa looked scornful.

Often, Ida wanted to tell Maud of the things she remembered. Telling made Uncle and New Zealand real. But even when Maud didn't say "fib", and enacted the part of willing listener, she didn't appear to take much interest. She never offered confidences in return. Perhaps being twelve years old made a difference. And there was, of course, the distressing fact of her virtue.

When a governess began coming, and they did lessons at the nursery table, Maud kept up her pose of perfect listener. She feathered in the shadow just right when she drew the Jonathan apple in free-hand; she got "The Charge of the Light Brigade" to heart in record time. Maud could sew a fine seam and play the violin. She was never plagued by an attack of the fidgets, sitting rock-like through each day's quota of *The Wide, Wide World*.

Elizabeth Wetherell was even worse, as authoress, than Mrs Walton, who thought up fearsome Old Grumpy in *Nobody Loves Me*. When, after *Wide World*, they started on *Queechy*, Ida resolved to have her revenge. She borrowed the horrid title for the name of her newest doll. Dolly had power even then. "Queechy" stopped sounding horrid ... the saintly Elfie continued praising Jesus, but the plot she featured in gathered pace.

Now, despite her painted face being faded and her head as bald as an egg, Queechy was Ida's friend. She talked to her a lot and sometimes Queechy talked back.

The night after Uncle's letter came inviting them to holiday, Ida couldn't sleep. "New Zealand, New Zealand," she whispered fiercely into the doll's slippery porcelain ear. This time, though Ida whispered so long that the words merged together and it sounded as if she said "Museum", Queechy chose to keep mum.

2

Of course, Blanche got her way. It was easy, all she had to do was indulge George, just a little. It wasn't too awful. She kept thinking how grateful he'd be in the morning. Afterwards — back in her night-gown, the nasty deed done — even as George snored beside her, she felt she belonged to herself.

Poor George. He'd looked sad as they boarded the ship; so sad that Blanche had suffered as much from guilt as sea-sickness all the way to Melbourne, and started disliking him again.

But by Sydney she was almost sorry she'd left. A dreadful melancholy descended — it was somehow the fault of the leaping waves. The further they pushed her from George, the stranger she felt. As if she wasn't sure who she was; as if she belonged to no one, not even herself. It was nonsense, of course. Might she never travel in a P. & O. steamer again. It was nothing, really. Only that the stewards were far from civil to the passengers who came but short distances. And she didn't like the table — eleven courses to dinner! And the smell of steam on the *Valetta* was very bad.

Only Harry could have dragged her away. He'd been favourite bro' from early on. One day, once upon a time, they'd caught the excursion train and left dirty Liverpool behind. She held Harry's hand and they tramped through streams and ended up in a meadow. Harry picked buttercups and threaded their stalks together. He crowned her Queen of the May, and she felt like a proper English girl at last, like one of the clean pink girls pictured on the frontispiece of the Christmas annuals.

Harry was fanciful, even then. "You and I together, Bets," he said. "You and I, Betsy, we are different." And he told her about the land across the sea. A new land where things were fresh, and people had a chance. He left out the heat and flies. He said, "We could do anything, once we got there. You believe me, don't you, Bets?" He said she was pretty enough for anything to happen. He smoothed her cheek and she started to believe him. She had never loved anyone more.

She had made him happy and on the way home they sang, and she put her head out of the train window and felt the wind on her face — it was wonderful . . . It had been terrible when, in the new land, he'd had to sail away. The swindle wasn't Harry's fault, not really. "Chin up," he had said and she'd gone back to the millinery shop to concentrate on chip-straw and Alsatian bows; her eyes had been red for days, but she'd kept on believing. And God was good. She'd borrowed one of the new season's ostrich-trimmeds for church, and contrived to share George's hymn-book. It wasn't a pick-up when you met at Holy Trinity. His brougham had dainty fringes to its blinds, and he tongue-kissed the tips of her fingers. Of course, she had to leave the milliner's while he introduced her to society, and veil the more distant past in discreet mystery, too. But it was easy, as Blanche, to pretend innocence; too easy, with George, to keep her knees pressed together. After a while he seemed to believe in his invention (almost as much as she did). And he never knew about the others, but called her his little queen. Which made her think of that first time, down among the buttercups. Oh, if only George had been Harry.

Poor Mama had headaches all the way to Sydney. It was the responsibility being too much for her, and feeling sea-sick, and her nerves. But the little girls had a lovely time on the *Valetta*. They were favourites on board and had every attention that hearts could wish.

Maud sang at a concert given by the passengers. She sang "Twickenham Ferry" and was enthusiastically encored. Then she did "Gin a body kiss a body" and brought down the house. The captain opined it the gem of the evening and told Mama next morning that the chief engineer was frantic about it, he was so delighted.

Cap's black servant was adept at reading heads. He reckoned Ida's to be very fine, and assured her she would prosper in life.

They steamed on and on. Glenelg seemed far away.

In Melbourne, where they stopped off, they saw the bronze statue of Burke and Wills, and Mr Cole's celebrated Book Arcade where literature was supplemented with trick mirrors and monkeys, a fernery and a five-piece orchestra.

Before Sydney, Mama's head was bad, but she came up with them to see the harbour. What a sight it was — like fairyland. The luncheon bell rang as they drew close, but they preferred the view to lunch.

Tier upon tier, the windows of old Sydney looked down upon them; then the steamer rounded Dawes' Point and the shore was thick with jetties and the bold forms of various craft. Then there were the screams of whistles and the clang of signal bells and the decks were alive with the bustle of departure.

There was a hansom from the wharf, and Ida saw little twisty streets and Chinamen, and sniffed hopefully for poppy fumes on the air. But soon the waterfront was left behind and respectability reigned: home was the Oxford Hotel, where you sat on the balcony to catch a cool breeze and watched the Woolloomooloo buses pass down King Street every five minutes.

They had the balcony and a private sitting-room and private meals, but Mama was horrified at the Oxford's charges — two pounds a day seemed exorbitant. And didn't she hate pianos. The hotel boasted a music-room, and someone was always pegging away at the same waltzes they'd hammered out on the *Valetta* from morning to night. And Mama's bed was about the brick-battest she'd ever slept on, though as it was intensely hot perhaps a hard bed was best.

It was December, and Papa would spend Christmas alone. Soon they would be with Uncle Harry and Aunt Cissie in New Zealand. Auntie had fallen mysteriously ill; Uncle was near his wits' end with worry. A steamer left for Auckland the day of their arrival, but Mama felt too queasy to venture on board. They would take passage, instead, by the *Ringarooma* which sailed on Thursday.

Sydney meant dust and a strong north wind. In spite of it, Mama dosed herself with Saline and took them to the Botanic Gardens. They saw sago-trees from Brazil and the giant palm by the rustic bridge. Mama led them over a carpet of buffalo-grass along Lovers' Walk, where shaded knolls commanded views of the cove. In the distance Government House rose up like a baronial castle; by the sea-wall was Mrs Macquarie's Chair, from which they surveyed the harbour.

They returned to the hotel for a nice tepid bath and, after tea, they felt fit as fiddles and not tired at all — which was good, as Papa's friend Mr Perry was to escort them on a stroll along George Street.

When they got there, Maud and Ida stared about in wonder. All the metropolitan multitude seemed to be assembled, marching in solemn procession. Mr Perry pointed out ebony-tinted Arab boys who'd strolled up from ships lying alongside the quay, and slant-eyed Chinamen come in from their vegetable gardens, and blackfellows from Queensland brought down to the city on a droving trip. There was a blind beggar with medical certificates and scriptural texts pinned to his lapels, and Mama gave them each a penny for his box. By the steps of the

Post Office was a crippled fiddler, scraping away at forgotten tunes.

Mr Perry seemed an unlikely friend for Papa to have. He wore check trousers and a ring on his little finger; he chewed Yankee Doodle plug. But Mama appeared to like him. She said it was a delight to be attended by a gentleman again, and linked his arm. Away from home, Mama was different: fluttery, all the time licking her lips as if she was nervous. But, as their promenade continued, Mr P. improved. He took them to some open ground near the Haymarket and they rode on the merry-go-round and watched jugglers toss coloured balls in the air; but decided to forgo the pennyworths of electricity that were sold to those who liked the sensation of shock.

Suddenly rain began pouring down and Mr Perry gallantly proffered his umbrella, which they scudded under back to the Oxford. Mr P. was soaked and, after Mama rang for tea, she laughed and said he might remove his damp jacket.

Mr Perry visited every day. Mama called him Tom, but she didn't smile at him so often. Thursday was almost come; soon Auckland would be real not Sydney. And Mama had changed her mind about the city's merits. The smells were enough to knock you down, and Adelaide could cut capers round it in the cab line. The hotel provided only bread and cheese for lunch, and port wine was eight shillings a bottle. The heat was intense, she'd been in a vapour bath since they arrived; and Tom was a dictatorial wretch, an idiot. He had a vile temper and Mama didn't care if he *had* looked after them and would see them off — it hadn't cost him a penny.

Mr Perry had fallen so far from grace that Mama said they were never to mention his name to Papa. But when their luggage had to be got from the Oxford to the wharf she began smiling again, and Mr Perry saw to the arrangements. He kissed Mama's cheek when he said goodbye, and presented them with a basket of fruit for the voyage. Ida almost pitied him, as, check-trousered and chewing hard, he stood in for Papa and waved them off on the *Ringarooma*.

Which was a smaller ship than the *Valetta* and rolled most dreadfully. It was fearsomely hot when they left, but before they got to the Heads it was blowing hard and they rolled about as if they were in a tub. They went down when the dinner gong sounded, but not to dinner.

All that night the noise on board was tremendous. Everything that wasn't tied was flying and sliding about; heavy seas came over the poop and several times water poured into the Ladies' Saloon. Mama slept in the top bunk and had to hold herself from being thrown out. But there were two stewardesses, both so attentive and kind that, although she rolled badly and they were so ill, they liked their trip by the *Ringarooma* — which ought to be *Ringarolla* — better than in the *Valetta*.

By Monday they had stopped rolling and it was pleasant on deck. About two o'clock they saw the first of New Zealand, the Three Kings rocks. From that time till they got in on Tuesday morning, they were close to land.

Rocks and mountains were all about them and, as they steamed into the harbour, Ida grew excited. Mama said the approach was grand and more beautiful, even, than Sydney's. And the air was so fresh and pure, the country so green and English.

3

They were arriving on the *Ringarooma* today. Already the waggonette stood ready to leave for the harbour. Harry was happy today because they were coming — she would let him be happy. In any case, Harry's moods changed so rapidly. Confronted by reality, a fleshly Blanche Dean at his side, he wouldn't stay happy for long. Harry had developed a conscience. He had worried so much about Cissie. "It is a judgment," he said. "If she should die I will blame only myself." But Cissie had miraculously grown better. It was good of Tempe to let her recover.

They were coming. She knew the day to be different when she awoke. The pine-trees and ancient volcanic hills loomed close; the pohutukawas were aflame with scarlet blossom; the secret pool was guarded by its tangle of willow and thorn — all the real world was as usual, but she had stopped being safe. She hated change; hated the Tempe, so carefully-buttoned, Harry would usher forward. Miss

Wimperis, my wife's half-sister, he'd say and it would be a lie. Tempe was nothing to do with the spineless creature who stank of ipecacuanha wine and mustard poultice; who lay on her bed once a month. Who lately had lain there more often.

Poor Cissie, perhaps she would die. Shall I let her? considered Tempe idly. And felt better. It was the day: they would come, but it hardly mattered. Her mountain was still there; Mount Eden they called it, but she knew it had another name . . . but forgotten, forgotten, and who am I?

. . . Mother had a woven flax basket. Together, they would stoop and search for treasures to fill it: puriri berries and the bigger, orangey karaka ones — ripe karaka flesh could be eaten raw though it tasted rather of turpentine, but the kernels had to be soaked and steamed to remove the poison. You must be careful with karaka, Mother said. And there were sticky mistletoe berries and the strange fruit of the titoki — curious, taking a year to ripen; split open down one greenish side to reveal the shiny black seeds sitting in the red, wrinkled pulp. But sometimes they did not venture so far. Mother was Linda and wore her silk dress; they turned from the forest to the rose-garden, and the basket filled up with bloated heads and a thick wave of scent. Father was content, then, when they sat on the verandah and spread pot-pourri petals on a tray. Mother was Linda and belonged to him. All her crinkled hair was coiled away. Mother was almost the proper English lady her benefactors had tried to make her, and Cissie watched from the cane lounge and her eyes snapped with hate.

Her name was not really Linda. She was not

English; she belonged to the old magic race. Though a moneyed family had given her their name and sent her to school in London; though she had an eighteen-inch waist and snow fell and frost tried to chill the magic away, they could not succeed. She was a beauty, even by their standards; she danced at Government House and attended afternoon teas and euchre parties; she married Mr Wimperis — but, really, they could not tame her. Days always came when she loosened the velvet snood and pulled out the hair-pins, and was herself in an old print frock. She seized Tempe's hand and they ran from the house barefoot, and under the beech-trees, among the ferns and the hooded orchids, she talked of giants and fairies and the nanakia who lived in the tree-tops and feasted on birds. Tempe would see their long fingernails which they used as spears, and the downy piles of feathers from the birds they had plucked, but she was not afraid — not then. The flax basket would fill up with berries, and Mother would not be Linda, but . . .

Forgotten. Mother died and everything changed. Father was only a man who wished to die, too; Tempe forgot the old words, even her mother's name. The forest accused her: for a while she would keep to the house, practise the soothing pianoforte airs, construe another world from the books in Father's library. But she could not forget entirely. There was always a time when she walked under the trees again.

Tempe was as much a half thing as Linda. The old knowledge still surfaced. It was better if she could be alone. Since Father had died and she had come to live at Epsom it was worse. Cissie had hated Linda, Father's second wife.

Poor Cissie. Doctor had been baffled by her sickness. Though, recently, the symptoms had abated. Though not in time to stop Harry's letter. Today they would come. Harry was whistling as the waggonette started off.

❦

Uncle Harry was on the wharf to meet them, and had his waggonette there to bring them home. It was a lovely drive from town to Epsom. Every few moments you caught a glimpse of the harbour, different little bits of it.

Auckland was different from Adelaide. The houses were only of wood... though they were built so prettily and looked so clean. After a while the horses left them behind and they were in the country. The air was crisp and everything was green. Mama said the fields might have been covered with a soft velvet carpet.

"It is like England," she said and squeezed Uncle's hand. She thought it the most pictures-que place she ever saw, except the Lakes and Derbyshire. Mama was bright and happy. She wore the kauri-gum heart at her throat.

They drove on, and everything was as Uncle's letters promised. There was the garden circled by pine-trees. And the house with its balcony and wide verandah, and Aunt Cissie running out to welcome them.

But she shouldn't have done that. Auntie was supposed to be sick — or had Uncle told a fib so

Papa might let them come? Hanging up her clothes in the new bedroom she shared with Maud, Ida pondered. There was another strange thing, too. Exchanging a hut on a gum-field for a flash house and Aunt Cissie and race-horses seemed to have changed Uncle Harry completely. The gentleman who'd met them at the wharf was nothing to do with the perfect being Ida remembered. She felt confused. At Glenelg, looking forward to New Zealand, she had seen Uncle Harry clearly.

The man who walked about downstairs was someone else. His clothes were so sober they would have suited a Methodist minister. He still had the strong tanned hands and the black hair, but he didn't have the dimple in his chin — you couldn't see his chin at all, for he covered it up with a beard. Uncle's beard was tickly when he kissed you; it was frizzy and didn't suit his mouth. His lips were two pale worms in the beard and, though Aunt Cissie was providentially recovered, his lips didn't laugh.

Though, really, Ida thought — as she left the muddle of unpacking to gaze out of the window — she must have remembered him wrongly. For Mama had greeted him straight away with "Harry"; she had run up to him and buried her face in his shoulder. She recognized him, she said he was the same old Harry — to a pin, even though he had the beard. And it was ridiculous to imagine Uncle unhappy. He had been pleased with the carved emu egg they had brought him as a memento of Australia. He smiled now and then; sometimes he whistled.

The window presented a most wonderful view, so grand that Ida wanted everything to be perfect to match it. You looked out over the garden to see, towering a little way off, various lofty hills that, perhaps, were even mountains. She had reached the dreamland at last. Aunt Cissie might have a screwed-up face and a hobby of painting seascapes on large oval pebbles (there were specimens of her art in every room); there might be the same Worcester china dessert plates as there were at home and a stuffy smell in the dining-room, but Ida knew that somewhere in those inky-green hills would be all that the geographical reader promised.

The drawing-room was comfortable and, like the Worcester plates, might have been twin to theirs at Glenelg. Mama and Uncle sat together on the sofa, and they each had so much to tell of. Auntie talked, too, as she presided over the tea-tray — she had a funny voice, squawky; she talked like a cockatoo. But she was kindness itself. And though she wasn't the invalid they'd expected, she was far from well. The pain was now and then severe, she said; she still tired easily.

Miss Tempe Wimperis was Auntie's half-sister — a young lady between seventeen and eighteen, a very nice amiable girl. She had been part of Uncle's household for several years, yet he'd made no mention of her in his letters. Ida liked her straight away, but it was Maud who drew Tempe's attention. She seemed fascinated by the resemblance she bore to Mama, remarking on it often during the evening.

Tempe, herself, despite a dowdy made-over dress, was comely enough. She had a pointed goldeny face and glossy black hair. Ida, always stirred by beauty, admired her more and more.

Auntie, on the other hand, seemed jealous of her sister's looks. Irritation lent her a little spirit. She drooped less within the cocoon of her vicuna shawl. Her tea-cup rattled in its saucer, she set it down with such force.

Uncle was courteous enough to Tempe, but distant, yet she didn't seem to mind. She couldn't have been nicer to the little girls. When the tea things were cleared away she offered to show them the garden.

Outside, it looked as if rain approached. Over the hills the sky was marbled with threatening cloud; the air was as fresh and crisp as it was sometimes at Mount Lofty, where Papa had taken them last summer to escape the heat of Glenelg. Everything was still; the flowers might have been painted in enamel, they gleamed out so precisely.

As they followed Tempe round the flower-beds, their feet dragged clumsily on the gravel path. That was wrong. The stillness, the pearly hydrangeas, the rose bushes bowed down by their swags of blossom, made Ida want to tiptoe, as if she was in church. This wasn't the New Zealand she'd dreamed of at home — this garden might have been English — but, in its own way, it was as perfect as the view from the window. The wind blew, and a heavy cloying scent, the wedding-day scent of orange-flower, was everywhere, mixed with a sharper smell from the pines. The pine-trees sheltered the garden in an arc and there were other trees, too. "Native trees," said Tempe proudly: shiny-leaved lacebarks; the Christmas-tree, whose proper name was pohutukawa.

"It's beautiful," Maud breathed reverently, and

Ida wished she had thought to say it first. Maud always did everything right. She looked so pretty, gazing at a clump of geraniums as if she'd never seen the flower before. But, curiously, Tempe didn't appear appreciative. "It is Cissie's garden," she said scornfully, curling her lip, "and this is Cissie's rockery."

The rockery was almost a relief after so much floral perfection. For it was ugly. Those gloomy little rocks, balanced carefully one atop the other, were strangely sinister, as were the plants that grew among them. Some resembled giant starfish; the worst one of all was just a bunch of crinkle-edged spears. "Cissie's aloe," said Tempe, and moved on across the tennis-lawn to point out the coachman's cottage.

The storm broke when they were in bed. Maud went on breathing regularly across the room, but Ida lay awake listening to the thunder. She couldn't remember ever hearing such rain; it was like goblins' fingers drumming on the roof.

Night had turned everything in the room un-familiar. The blurred shape of the wardrobe seemed to stand where the chest-of-drawers was before Maud blew out the candle. And Ida's bed was un-comfortable. It was one of those chain ones, and the mattress was too big, its sides lapped over and she feared she'd slip to the floor.

Why had they come? Auntie was crabby . . . the powder she pretended not to use made her face look dusty. And, yes, Ida knew Uncle to be unhappy. At home, Papa said grace, too, but not like Uncle, whose voice quivered and broke fiercely, as if the words really mattered and he was determined that God shouldn't overlook the fact they were said.

It was horrid here; New Zealand was a fraud . . . Ida had almost decided to push her way into Maud's bed — Maud would let her, Maud was good — when she remembered Queechy.

The strange floorboards creaked as she felt her way towards the valise where the doll still lay from the voyage, unthought of till now. Then it was better. The goblins' fingers kept up their din, the chain bed was still dangerous, but Ida's friend would keep her from harm.

4

They sat on the balcony, and Mama prodded her needle at summer muslin. The dress was for Tempe, but Mama sewed it as much for Aunt Cissie. Aunt Cissie disliked Tempe: Mama disliked Auntie (the dress was a snub).

It was pleasant on the balcony. The rain that had so far marred each day had ceased, and they sat in a pool of sunlight. Mama bent her head and revealed the kiss-curls at her neck. Maud sucked on a pin and listened to the little sounds of her sewing — the soft tap of needle against thimble, the neat snap as Mama nipped off thread with her teeth. She felt perfectly happy, blissful. Happy, and virtuous, too. The letter written to dear Papa, alone at Glenelg in their absence, was ready for the afternoon's mail-boat; she'd saved Auntie's maid the trouble of turning her mattress, and brushed up her boots herself — she wore them now, nicely shined, their buttons resembling winking eyes. Thank goodness Mama dressed them in style; thank goodness Maud had silvery hair, brushed smooth and tied with a floppy bow, and that underneath the clothes was her body, as perfect as everything else.

Being twelve years old — nearly thirteen — was strange. Maud sat beside Mama on the balcony, and wondered if it was wicked to think as she did. The thoughts had only just begun; only lately had she lain awake at night, aware of her body as something precious. Oh, you are beautiful, Maud said to herself at night, and sometimes started to cry. She didn't know why. She felt happy as she cried . . . happy now . . .

To begin with, Mama worried about money. She opened her purse and counted its contents, and found the spon to have melted away. Papa must send her ten pounds more, if he didn't think it very dreadful. And she had made up her mind they couldn't afford Christmas cards this year, so he might advertise in the *Observer*: "No cards". Now they were with Harry and Cissie, though, laundry would be their only expense. They had everything they wanted in the way of dress; she was glad they'd purchased hankies and gloves in Melbourne — it saved any bother here, as they were four miles from town and Cissie seldom went in. She had two pounds left, so please would George send her a little more.

Ida read Mama's letter while she sewed on the balcony. Mama was not consistent, being one instant penny-pinch, the next spendthrift. Often Ida pitied her. Mama hinted that she had not enjoyed a pleasant childhood; she spoke dreamily, sometimes, of nasty things. Ida could not imagine Mama eating cold lumpy porridge for breakfast, or attending a school where the teachers sewed bags of sulphur into the hems of their skirts to outwit the vermin.

Mama only spoke of such improbabilities when Papa was not in the room. Her cheeks would flush and her voice grow high and excited.

But when she entertained ladies who called with tales of another childhood, spent largely abroad, Mama's voice sounded coldly indifferent. She reminisced with so little feeling, that they might have been merely another's experiences she'd cribbed from a book. Ida could never see Mont Blanc or Wiesbaden clearly.

When Mama told of matted hair and adenoids, of pretty girls turning to old women overnight, her voice was vivid and alive. Ida shivered, for she saw all the nasty untrue things exactly. Curiously, Mama sounded glad as she declared defiantly that you couldn't blame anyone for what they did; that life was not what it appeared. For a moment she looked at the little girls strangely, as if she bore them no relation — almost as if she disliked them. Then, just as suddenly, she was herself again — the Mama who said "There is a pattern" and "God is good". Who sat calmly in the drawing-room, occasionally stifling a yawn, as Ida dropped crumbs from her arrowroot biscuit on the hearth-rug and Maud tuned her violin.

Sometimes Mama's stories frightened Ida, for she thought they might even be true. But Maud allayed her fears. Maud assured Ida that Mama's stories were merely make-believe. She said Mama might have been an actress, if she wished, to rival Maggie Moore in *Struck Oil!*

But Ida suspected Maud to lack imagination. She went on half-believing. Because of her childhood, Ida thought, from time to time — particularly *this* time, so far from home — Mama splurged, then worried over cash. Because of it, though Mama's voice might win when the drawing-room door flew shut and they started to quarrel, Papa, who handled the purse-strings, was a victor, too. Away from Papa, Mama started to love him. Silly Mama. Why, she might have borrowed the money from Uncle Harry ... Though Mama was proud. And Ida suspected something to be wrong. Mama and Uncle had walked under the pine-trees, yesterday, talking gravely; afterwards, Mama sat pensive in her room.

Though perhaps it was only the fault of the motion of the ship. Mama complained she felt it still; that nothing was steady and solid, and she often turned giddy. But today she seemed better and said her head had not ached since she landed. Today, on the balcony, she hummed as she sewed at Tempe's dress.

So Ida forgot Mama's troubles and decided to explore the garden. But halfway down the stairs she paused. In the hall, opposite the table ranged with the candlesticks that lighted them to bed, was a large carved chest. Tempe stood beside it and, as Ida peeped through the banisters, she lifted its lid and drew out something white and ran with it on to the verandah.

Ida was disappointed when she looked in the chest. It held nothing more than a great many

31

garments, terribly old-fashioned. Everything was wrapped away in layers of brittle tissue-paper that crumbled under her fingers. There was a melancholy smell of ancient rose petals and camphor.

Ida shivered and, like Tempe, ran outside. Mount Eden and Mount St John stubbed a peacock-blue sky; the garden seemed brighter than ever.

Once past the coachman's cottage, you were surrounded by trees. Soon the pines grew so close together that they shut out the sky, and Ida knew she had entered a forest. But, though the pines cast a gloomy shade, she wasn't nervous, for nothing was foreign — she had entered countless such woods from the nursery's safety, by way of the pages of Grimm. Then, without warning, the forest turned to a jungle, and she walked through a tangle of glossy green. There was no light or shade, no illusion of depth. The delicate ferns at her feet, the garlands of jagged leaves which quite obliterated the trunks that bore them — all dazzled equally with the same harsh greenness.

Ida walked, unthinking, down a rough path that had been trodden through the ferns. Insects rose in a dotted cloud; once she thought she saw something pale moving before her. The path looped upward, then she was walking easily downhill and, again, everything changed. Now she walked through an overgrown English garden — a wilder, more romantic version of Aunt Cissie's. Hollyhocks and poppies, roses and a frothing mess of honeysuckle, were tangled in a thicket of thorn and bramble.

In places she was surprised by crumbling piles of stone and a mutilated company of antique gods and goddesses. Venus lacking more than her arms, Cupid without his bow — dappled with bird-droppings, kilted with creepers.

The garden appeared to be in a natural hollow, surrounded by high grassy banks. At the foot of one of these flowed a shallow stream and as Ida waded through it she noticed, half-hidden by trailing ivy, what seemed to be a small cave. But what she saw when she pushed aside the ivy was more than a trick of nature. For the walls of the cave were lined with shells. All about her were tidy rows of turret- and necklace- and cockle-shells, sting winkles and common whelks. In the centre of the cave was a low stone table, the legs of which were carved to resemble dolphins. On the table were folded a pair of drawers and a chemise, a pair of stays and a petticoat, a jacket-bodice and a skirt — decidedly, the articles of a young lady's rather skimpy summer costume. Under the table were a pair of buttoned boots, each with a stocking and a garter tucked neatly inside its toe.

Ida stared at the clothes in wonder, and then a noise broke through her reverie. She thought she heard someone singing. Quickly, she slipped through the ivy. But no sound came to her; nothing moved.

She went on following the stream, which now was arched with the branches of willows. And then she stopped, for the song had begun again. Before her was a bend in the stream and she left off paddling to climb towards it on the bank. The singing guided her. Stooping, feeling her way through the tasselled branches, she saw that the stream bent itself to become a pool. And in the pool,

33

massed about with thorn and willow and wild roses, something floated: Tempe.

Ida wanted to laugh. Tempe floated there, beautiful but ridiculous — her hair come out of its pompadour to fan her face; her white dress turned quite transparent. The pool was choked with star-grass and milfoil, so that she seemed to lie on a soft green meadow, that now and then rhythmically moved. In her hair she had stuck small white daisies; her hands were clasped on a bunch of them, too. And she lay there in the day-time, probably catching her death, without petticoats, in a dress so thinly transparent that it provided a regular peep-show. And she sang. But Ida couldn't understand a word. And, even as she watched, it grew worse and worse — better and better: Tempe floundered, then rose from the pool to wade to the bank, shrug off the dress and stand naked. Blushing, Ida tunnelled backward through the willows, to make for home.

5

Harry said, "We are pleased to have you here, Tempe. This is your home, now." He looked welcoming enough; it was Cissie who was the trouble. Cissie was a good sort, of course, a true Christian who did not shirk her duty, but: "There is something I cannot stomach about her," she confided to Mrs Hunt. Always had been — the same with Linda.

Father, newly widowed, did it to spite her. He banged down the whisky glass and said he didn't give a tinker's damn. At the next ball he did it again. Swept her away in the Lancers, filled up her programme: Waltz 2. *Come to my heart* ... Schottische 7. *I am Jack Jingle.* Cissie sat on alone as ever, behind a potted palm; beating time with her fan, hearing the chaperones' voices ... admiring Linda, hating her: "She is the season's sensation," said the vicar's wife, lowering her eye-glass. "Beautifully turned out," agreed the doctor's sister. "But would you like her for *your* son — as dark as that?" Though she was a pretty little thing, agreeable... Yet when Mildred saw her on Lambton Quay she passed her without a word. She seemed vague, sometimes. There was something — not quite right, do you think? "Only to be expected," said the vicar's wife, smugly. "Oh yes, I know we're all the same in the eyes of our Creator, but what is she, where does she fit in?" One must face facts — all the style in the world couldn't disguise it: she was neither one thing or the other. "Really, my dear, I pity her."

Linda danced with him. On and on. Satin shoes skimming the polished floor, muslin skirts flying behind her... past asparagus fern and azaleas, the band in the corner and all the white faces — proper English faces — judging her, hating. She whirled on and on: pretty Linda, in the arms of someone who was kind. "He is old enough to be your father," they scolded. But he bent his head and kissed her shoulders. She had remembered to powder them, and he said, "You smell of roses."

He was an old man, but: "I don't care," she said, the day he took her into his study. They'd looked at each other over their tea-cups; the spice cake was good, but she couldn't swallow. Though she only went into the study to see his American Indian pen-wiper, his Berlin black inkstand. She supposed what they did was pleasant. "I don't care," she had said, even though the sofa was narrow, and on the wall, framed in maplewood, was a memorial-card to his late dear wife. But he kissed her shoulders and said she smelled of roses. "I must have a needle and thread," she said later, for he had torn her new tailor-made in his haste.

He would pull out the invisible hair-pins, and her hair crinkled down and he called her his little savage, his dusky Eve. He was terribly English, then; when he paid her the compliments she didn't think him so kind.

But he loved her so much that he married her, and then Tempe was born and she died. Cissie married Major Harry Jones of Auckland. She almost stopped hating her father, for Wellington was far away. But then he died, too, and: "We are pleased to have you here, Tempe," said Harry. "This is your home."

It was awful at first, everything was strange. The hills in the distance frightened her; pines were dismal trees. The new bedroom might be furnished with odds and ends from Linda's old one, her chest might stand in the hall, but, because Tempe couldn't remember Mother's proper name, all the old things reproached her. She could hardly bear to see them.

Then Father's books arrived on a cart and went into Harry's library. One day Tempe walked through the door and she might have come home. Harry had Sir Walter Scott in marble on the mantel, Father had chosen Dante, but there were the same oriental vases and curtains of dark crimson rep, the same dear old books. She had forgotten those morocco covers and spines latticed with gilt and gold-leaf; the pages of other worlds that they enclosed.

You turned back a piece of tissue-paper and a poet surveyed you. Mr Browning had a crease between the eyes and a frothy beard. Mrs Hemans smirked above a double-strand of pearls. Samuel

Taylor was a disappointment, being merely pudding-faced; Percy Bysshe was best of all . . . till Tempe moved on to Alfred, Lord T., who fixed her with his dirty monk eyes.

His words lived up to his looks. She got them to heart without effort. "O Love, Love, Love! . . .", "Now sleeps the crimson petal, now the white . . ." — it was easy. She read on and on, the eye-strain over all that small print was worth it. For Cissie's malevolence dwindled to nothing as Tempe escaped her with Elaine, lily maid of Astolat and glossy-throated Isolt.

It was easy to dismiss a merely fleshy enemy, but a dead one was a different matter. For, though Tennyson helped, he couldn't shut Linda out. She usually came at night. She squeezed her way beneath Tempe's counterpane, she got right under the sheets. And her ghostly mouth clamped on Tempe's ear. "Forgotten, forgotten," she moaned, and the words wormed into Tempe's brain; they surfaced behind her eyelids to conjure up pictures: Mother with her flax basket, gathering titoki berries in the forest — a pretty picture until you looked close . . . for her hands had turned to claws; skeleton fingers held the basket. "Look at me," Mother commanded. "Why do you live and not I?"

Then, one day, pacing Cissie and Harry's real wood, Tempe took a different path. The pines petered out, the ratas and tree-ferns began; she came to the overgrown garden with its grotto and pool. It was there, among the willows and wild roses that Shalott and its Lady became real. Tempe had never cared for her — mooning from her casement — before. But, under the willows she read the poem again and, as the Lady sang her last song, Mother sang, too. Tempe listened and smiled, for this time Linda was at peace. Her hands on the flax basket were fleshly, and they put the basket down and stroked Tempe's hair, and wreathed it with ivy leaves and daisies.

Then Tempe must go down to the pool; she must wade right in and float among the weeds in her petticoat. It was like praying, really. You left identity behind, you looked up at the sky and everything merged. All your problems were solved; you knew who you were.

In the water Tempe felt herself go free. She was the Lady and she was Linda and she was also herself. Parakeets keened overhead — she floated in a North Island pool, but she also floated down to Camelot; she floated under an English, as well as an antipodean sky. All the trappings of the legends merged, too. Willow and thorn and wild rose were neatly muddled with titoki and flax basket and Mother's voice telling the old names... Tempe opened her mouth, and Mother told of nanakia, the goblins who lived in the trees, and of the turehu and patu-paiarehe, those seldom-seen fairy folk. Tempe sang a song, and no one knew the words but she and Linda.

It didn't matter that, as she waded from the pool, the words drifted away; that, as she came out from the shadow of the pines, they were quite gone. In a sense, the forgetting was good. Her secret world stayed separate from Cissie's smug kingdom of tea-cup and crumb cloth.

Tempe would return refreshed, but it was a nuisance to have a wet petticoat (she couldn't float without it, for that would be cheating — the Lady floated poetically, robed in snowy white). Then Linda kindly nudged Tempe's memory and reminded her of the dress inside the chest. It was the muslin she'd worn when she'd first danced with Father, and the sun would dry its dampness in a trice.

Floating in the pool, Tempe somehow placated the pine-trees and the ancient hills. All the natural world became a friend. One day, soon, she would climb to the top of Mount Eden. Up there, she would be stronger than ever.

She had been strong for ages, now. Though, occasionally, the calm left her. Harry, for instance, had upset her, so she had to take her revenge. It was always people who ruined things. She dreaded their coming, Cissie's afternoons-at-home were a torment. And then she'd sickened too fast, and Harry had panicked, and bid Blanche Dean and the little girls to cross the Tasman. Funny . . . Blanche and Ida and Maud — Tennyson had addressed lines to them, too. Maud was the image of her mama. Maud might prove useful if Harry hurt Tempe even more; if Blanche Dean decided to claim him.

※

Uncle Harry had a letter-box fastened to his gate, and one morning the children found Christmas cards in it — beautiful gelatine cards in boxes, come all the way from Papa.

Uncle's friend, Mr Maufe, had been invited to stay over Christmas. He was a fine old gentleman; such a handsome, nice old man. He played the flute

40

very well, and in the evenings he and Maud and Tempe played as a trio. The violin and piano and flute sounded well together, and sometimes Mama would sing.

Mr Maufe always stayed with Uncle and Auntie when he came to town. He lived somewhere about the hot springs, and his wife was an artist like Aunt Cissie, and he had a son, also very clever, and two daughters. Poor Mr Maufe, Auntie told Mama,was brought up to consider himself heir to Lord Fermoy in Ireland, but Lord F. married late and had a son, and of course put Mr Maufe's nose out of joint.

In the garden at Glenelg there was a lovely double red and white fuchsia, and there was one in Aunt Cissie's garden, too. On Christmas morning Maud and Mama picked some sprays and made bouquets for the table.

They had a merry dinner and drank Papa's health. Uncle Harry seemed brighter since Mr Maufe's arrival. Suddenly he was a great tease, and full of fun.

Mr and Mrs Hunt ate with them, too. Mrs Hunt was Aunt Cissie's special friend. She was a little high-bosomed lady, rosy and polished; she was a Jewess. Auntie told Mama about that, too. Ida listened and thought it romantic — how Mr Hunt married Miss Isaacs, and her family went into mourning as if she'd died, and Mr Hunt ceased being in the best society. But when she saw them across the dinner table they seemed ordinary. Mr Hunt spilled wine on his waistcoat and picked up his turkey bones with his fingers; Mrs Hunt had inquisitive eyes.

She and Aunt Cissie talked and talked. They

didn't like Tempe, it was plain to see, even though she looked so nice in the dress that Mama had sewn her. Mr Maufe, however, kissed the tips of his fingers when Tempe appeared at table. It was an Empire dress, low-cut, that Mama had sewn — a copy of the costume of ancient Greece. Tempe had left off her corsets to suit its style, and her chest moved up and down loosely, differently from the other ladies'. Perhaps it was this that caused Aunt Cissie and Mrs Hunt to shake their heads.

But Mr Maufe decidedly approved. And even Mr Hunt, who dropped a hot potato in his lap, he looked so long when she leant forward to pass him the cruet-set; even Uncle Harry.

But Mama didn't take heart from all these compliments to her handiwork. She toyed with her turkey; she hardly touched her wine. Perhaps she was merely modest. Though it might have been the fault of Aunt Cissie.

For, as Auntie cast off the effects of her illness, she grew more lively. She didn't stop talking, and her voice was so loud you could plainly hear her all over the house. Oh yes, she was kind, Mama supposed . . . but so fussy she made you feel you should like to run away and hide, often and often. And when Mama finished Tempe's dress, even when Tempe wore it, Auntie didn't say thank you. And, truth to tell, Cissie was one of the greatest scandal-mongers Mama ever was with. "It seems a great failing here," she wrote to Papa, "and you know how I hate it. It is a very small place, this Auckland."

Ida was happy when she read of Mama's feelings, for now she disliked Auntie, too. When she'd come back from watching Tempe in the pool, she'd been excited, and wanted to tell someone. She started to tell Auntie, who only said: "Oh be quiet, child. I have other things to think of." So Ida retreated to the bedroom to whisper in Queechy's ear.

Mama's letters grew better all the time. "My dear old darling," the next one commenced, "Perhaps I expected too much, perhaps I am sick for a sight of you — but, whatever the reason may be, I am bitterly disappointed in everything here except the country which is, beyond description, lovely."

They did not sit up to see the new year in — the first time Mama remembered not doing so. But, she told Maud and Ida later, she woke at twenty minutes to one and put her head out of the window and blew Papa her first kiss of 1885, and the little girls her second. Now Mama had Papa's likeness displayed in her room — the one of him sitting on the rustic seat, smoking his pipe.

The summer had regularly set in, and it was hot. There'd only been three days without rain since they arrived, so it was a different heat to Adelaide's. Mama thought it both trying and relaxing. The sun was powerful and, despite hats and parasols, they were all more sunburnt than they ever were at home. But they never had Adelaide's hot north winds and the evenings were cool, often quite cold, and there was always a heavy dew.

The evenings were given up to music in the drawing-room. Mr Maufe really understood the flute, and played from sight.

Mr Maufe, like Tempe, had taken a fancy to Maud. Though she was twelve years old, he — poor old gentleman — seemed to think her the same age as Ida. It was the jest of the house, the way he petted her so sweetly and delighted to run his fingers through her hair. His pet name for Maud was Master Bob, and after Christmas dinner, when they all squeezed into the waggonette for a tour of the local beauty spots, Mr Maufe bade Bob sit on his knee. Ida had to make do with Uncle's.

But with Auntie it was drive, drive, drive: she let no one rest, she was a regular Tartar to her servants. Mama unlocked her portable writing desk and worked out her temper on paper:

". . . Her housemaid left on Friday and a new one comes tomorrow and we have worked like Britons doing housemaid's work between us. Yesterday, Cook being poorly, we did hers as well. I made four beds with Maud and Ida's help; I brushed the hall, dusted the smoking- and dining-rooms, and boiled the eggs for breakfast. We all helped clear away and then I washed up while Maud and Tempe wiped, and then I came upstairs and tidied the bed-rooms . . ."

Then Cook said she was leaving, and Aunt Cissie ran a splinter down her nail and complained without cease — it was the final straw. Mama told Uncle that they must go.

"I get," Mama said, "some very homesick feelings sometimes." New Zealand's landscape was glorious, and its climate, too, but she wondered how the garden at Glenelg was looking . . . and if the ponies were all right, and dear old Bo'. "Cissie is quite recovered from her illness — there is no worry now, on that count. And" — here Mama's mouth twisted, her voice sounded bitter — "I only see you at meals and in the evening, Harry. And you are leaving for

Christchurch tomorrow." (Uncle Harry's horses were to run in Christchurch in the midsummer handicap.)

Ida could have cried. For so long she had dreamed of their coming. They had come, and already she had discovered a secret garden, and seen Tempe without her clothes, and Auntie said you could climb to the top of Mount Eden — she wanted to climb it. She didn't like Auntie and she had started to miss Papa, but there was so much else, yet, she wanted to see.

When Mama said they must go, Uncle didn't demur. It was plain to see he didn't want them.

Ida thought there was no hope, when Mr Maufe saved the day. Somehow he had overheard. He strode into the room, and his poor old hands were trembling. He was as agitated as that, he cared so much.

"Oh no, no, no," cried Mr Maufe. "You cannot think of leaving New Zealand yet, Mrs Dean." Why, rarely did Mr Maufe meet a lady of such charm as Mama, and how could she be so cruel as to cheat him of her company? And her little girls were sweethearts, and Master Bob most wonderfully musical (something should be done for Master Bob's music). Oh no, no, no — they couldn't go. Why, that very day Mr Maufe had planned to invite them — Mama, Ida, Bob — to visit him at his home in the country. The Peach Groves (that was the name of Mr Maufe's estate) was a long way off, near the hot springs at Te Aroha. "You will see a different North Island there, dear lady," said Mr Maufe, wheedling. "Up there is a district which contains

45

the most extraordinary scenery on the face of the globe."

Te Aroha was a fashionable place — people went there for the baths. "Aroha" was the Maori word for love, and The Peach Groves sounded poetic. Mr Maufe was related to Lord Fermoy, and knew the nephew of the Earl of Annersley intimately. Mama nodded her head.

That night they had an hour's music — Maud on the violin, Mr Maufe on his flute and Tempe accompanying. They played "Ehren on the Rhine", "Believe me if all those endearing young charms" and several others. Mr Maufe took the air, and Tempe played an accompaniment with her left hand and the contralto part with her right, and Maud took tenor on the violin. It sounded so well.

6

He was a good old man.

He was bad, the very devil, and not so ancient, either. A few wrinkles and a bald pate signified little — he was young, still; a day still came when he had to get away. The solitude drove him wild . . . and Wifey's artistic faculty, the boy's endlessly thumping thumb, the girls' sad noses. Those girls had let him down. They'd grown from rosy cherubs, just the sort he liked, to good dull women. They'd never marry now, but keep on snapping lily stalks — taming the long-tongued calla lilies into fit tributes to their Willy-wetleg Jesus.

Ethel and Queenie did the flowers at church. And, wistfully, they knitted booties for other people's dear little babies. And, wincing, fought the grey in their hair with iron rations and a head-rub of cheap claret. They were pale women, thirtyish, who thought of themselves as girls. Ethel was a Woollenite, faithful to Dr Jaegar's sanitary notions (she wore digitated hosiery and combinations of

47

stockinette). Queenie was a little bit greenery-yallery, with a protruding upper lip and an aesthetic tea-gown. Ethel now and then wrote verses and, as "Tea Rose" or "An Old Subscriber" sent them off to the *Girl's Own Paper*. Queenie fought a bit harder and sometimes frizzed her fringe (the usual story, Queenie's: young man killed on the North-West frontier in the Afghan fighting of 1880).

Octavius, now — a nice enough lad, though his head was a trifle large and he had a habit of flexing his thumb. The thing was this way — Oc would sit down in his chair and cross his legs neatly and clasp his hands and start smiling and do it. He would thump and thump. Rhythmically, that supple digit would rise and fall. Sometimes he did it fast, sometimes slow; always it was his right-hand thumb he exercised: that thumb was abnormally large and swollen-tipped.

Poor Oc . . . though it might have been worse. If he did have habits worse than thumbing he kept them a secret. Up in his work-room he toiled without cease. It had started as a hobby — postage stamps, birds' eggs and butterflies didn't interest the boy in the least, but he took to bookbinding like a natural. He started with Ethel's broken-backed prayer-book and progressed to his papa's collection. He did wonders with loose fly-leaves, foxed pages, sloppy stitching; he could produce an elegantly marbled endpaper or a floral sprig in gold leaf easy as winking; he stitched with fairy fingers.

It was handy that Octavius had his hobby, for his papa couldn't resist a good read. And every time things got too much (Wifey's art, Oc's habit, the girls' goodness), became so bad that a book couldn't soothe him, Mr Maufe took off. It was lucky he had struck up acquaintance with Harry Jones, for in Auckland, now, he was spared hotel bills. Though old Harry had rather fallen off on the last couple of visits — he was melancholy company, lately. Though a bit more spirit to the man at Christmas dinner. But who wouldn't be spirited, fronting Miss Tempe?

Travelling offered compensations. Auckland might be countrified, but it could offer civilized pleasures. Mr Maufe knew a certain little door . . . Amy's lips were sealing-wax red and just as sticky; Eileen might have come straight from the convent with her forelock tied up with baby ribbon, and all those scapulas safety-pinned to her chemise.

But books were best. A thrill at second-hand was somehow tastier, lasted longer, could be proceeded with at the desired pace. For Mr Maufe had particular tastes; they weren't commonplace books he purchased. Not that merely any uncommon book would do; Mr Maufe's purchases being the aristocracy of their sort. Indeed, he had a horror of the usual variety of smudged illustration and blotting-paper texture of page; the type set so hastily that it bled at the corners and frightened itself off margin. Decidedly, Mr Maufe's books were masterpieces of their kind: dainty little items, beautifully got up in vellum or silk, with best-woven pages and illustrations so exquisite that you didn't miss a detail. They were old books he liked — very old, and this was where Oc came in handy. For often, favourite pages flapped loose from all those years of close attention; sometimes a choice volume had suffered shamefully.

Oh yes, Mr Maufe knew a certain little shop . . . And, as well, old Harry's library was always good for perusal. For, high above *The Annual Register* and Tempe's poets was a shelf . . . Harry probably didn't even know they were there (Harry having accumulated his library in several hereditary job lots). Each time Mr Maufe mounted Harry's library ladder and reached out a hand, he wondered which long dead relative of Cissie's he should thank for the rare carnal pleasures he'd soon enjoy.

Harry's books made up for much. Cissie was hard to take, and though Harry could be jolly he did go on about his horses. But, of course, as well as books there was Tempe.

She was a strange one — at first Mr Maufe couldn't make her out. She was demure, yet with that hint of still waters running deep that he found attractive. He liked her so much that, one day when they were together in the library (she attending to her shelf, he to his), he stepped down from his ladder to kiss her cheek. And awful, awful — all she did was stand and laugh. Laughed at, Mr Maufe was no one — only Maufe major crying out his eyes in the big dorm at school . . . Mama was far away, and he couldn't help it, and all round him smaller boys sniggered — Maufe minor among them.

So Tempe became someone to admire. Someone you could allowably like because nothing was expected of you. She had laughed and, feeling awful, you shrank to pigmy size and she saw and knew what you were but, knowing, didn't judge you. Tempe and Mr Maufe became friends. Really, she was like a man. He respected her; he could read his books in her presence and now and then share with her a particular page, though his books never interested her much.

One day she said to him: "You aren't a person like the others — I mean a proper person like Cissie or Mrs Hunt. It's all right with you, I don't have to worry. Being with you is like being in the water with Mother. Though you're weak and she's strong."

Which didn't make sense, but somehow seemed complimentary. Mr Maufe smiled and said "Charmed, dear lady," and wondered how she was getting on with Harry. Something was up; he was sure of it. Lucky devil. Though no — having Tempe as a pal was so much better. Man to man, you could confide, and even a book couldn't give that relief. For instance, sometimes a chap was plagued by a lower order of desire, and it was good to tell how a book wouldn't do, not even the best, and he had to resort to Amy, though Eileen was better ... How, one day he might see a pretty little cherub without her mama in Queen Street or Karangahape Road ... How, one day he had come to spend Christmas with Harry and Cissie, and set eyes on Maud.

So they stayed on, and even though there was no chance of Maud continuing her violin lessons as they were so far from town, and Ida kept missing Papa, the little girls were glad. For there were lots of things to do. Now Aunt Cissie was better they started to meet society. Mama might shake her head and say: "Of all the slow people I ever met, commend me to the inhabitants of Auckland," but Maud and Ida found society entertaining.

They went to Lieutenant Colonel Charlton Mawson's garden party and to the Alexanders' musical evening where Maud sang "Golden Dove" and Ida, not to be left out, had a try at "When Sparrows Build". They attended a tennis party at Mr and Mrs Strettlers' (*he* was a nephew of a late Lord Chief Justice of Ireland, and an uncle of *hers* was once Governor of Victoria: Auckland was an aristocratic place!). Then there was Mrs Hunt's afternoon-tea party and, though their hostess's eyes were as treacherous as ever, the view from her verandah was striking — you could see all over the harbour; you saw the grand old mountain island of Rangitoto in the distance. Another time they took a boat across the harbour to North Shore to see through a sugar refinery. That was interesting enough, but the journey back was better. The wind was high and a rough sea made them move about, and Aunt Cissie was nervous and didn't bother to hide it. She was such an amusement to the other passengers, giving screams and declaring they were going down, that Uncle Harry told her not to be a fool. He spoke sharply, but Auntie didn't seem to care.

Uncle had returned from Christchurch happy, because Wapiti won the midsummer handicap. Uncle was now more like the gentleman Ida remembered, so nice that he resembled an angel. He wore his hat tipped back at an angle and his lips were no longer melancholy; he said grace in a regular voice. Though he didn't smell rankly of horse, it was easy to imagine him surrounded by the clatter of iron-shod hoofs and the cracking of whips.

Uncle was away south a lot. He kept his race-horses in Christchurch and wouldn't race them up north, because in Auckland there was so much dishonesty. Things were different down south, Uncle said, where racing was a gentleman's sport.

Racing was Uncle Harry's prime interest; they heard so much about it that Mama said, sarcastically, that they were getting quite *au fait* on the subject. ". . . But dear old hubby," she wrote to Papa, "I rejoice that you are not a racing man. It is Dead Sea fruit, and only causes weariness of spirit and lots of expense."

Mama didn't sound like Papa's Pepper-box now, nor did she seem like Uncle Harry's doting sister. She had exchanged his kauri-gum heart for the ruby-studded Maltese cross. Now Uncle was happy and Mama was not. One day Ida heard her talking to Tempe on the balcony.

Mama's tongue had turned as treacherous as Mrs Hunt's eyes. She sewed at the silly little wrap that would suit Tempe so beautifully, and said cruel things about her brother.

". . . He is so different to what I had imagined him," she finished, sighing. "He is so irritable whenever I speak to him — though perhaps that is caused by his headaches, perhaps they have flared up again. Harry used to suffer from rheumatic gout, once. He had rheumatic gout in his head and suffered most terribly."

Though she started out by disliking him, and said the cruel words, Mama's voice quickly turned sad and she'd talk of Uncle with pity. And end up by loving him till tomorrow came, and she hardly saw him.

". . . for he is nearly all day at the Club," she told her other confidant, Papa. "He is away, and we sit in the drawing-room, the windows of which are always kept closed, so that it is stuffy and hot and we stew there all afternoon."

Poor Mama must sit and sit. Even on Auntie's afternoons-at-home, for Cissie made the excuse that she was not strong enough to take her visitors into the garden. So Mama must sit cooped up, talking rot, while the children played tennis on the lawn with Tempe and Mr Maufe.

On and on would Mama's pen fly: "I hate Saturdays here! Their idea of hospitality is so funny compared to ours. For instance, last Saturday Lieutenant Colonel Charlton Mawson and Mrs Mawson came about three o'clock and stayed till past seven. Mrs Mawson had a cup of tea and the Colonel some claret, but they were not asked to stay to dinner, though they could see the cloth laid in the dining-room. About seven, Mrs Mawson rose to go and then Cissie said 'Oh, I don't like you going without dinner,' but never asked them to stay. I'm glad our ways are different, George. No wonder Adelaide people have a good name for hospitality."

Aunt Cissie did not keep a good table and, in Mama's opinion, was a poor housekeeper. She and Uncle spent an awful amount of money on their race-horses and got nothing for it.

But the little girls were happy. Dear Mr Maufe was a lovely friend to have. He always had a lolly in his pocket and was all the time offering to give you a piggy-back, as if you were merely an infant. He was old, but nice looking, with a ruddy complexion and a thin moustache that looked as if a line of sugar crystals had dropped above his lip by mistake. He had hairs coming out of his cuffs on to his hands, though: this wasn't so nice. And a funny thing was, too, that in the house with his spectacles on and his white hair flopping about, he looked kindly; but coming up the drive with his bell-topper on, without the specs, he looked different.

For, with his hat slicing off his dear old white head, you concentrated on Mr Maufe's face. And, really, it wasn't so nice when you came to think of it. Without their shields of pebble-glass, Mr Maufe's eyes were hard. Hatless, when he swung you about on the lawn and you chewed on his lolly, you hardly noticed it. But when he walked up from the waggonette with his parcel of books you did.

But in the library he wore his spectacles, and his hat hung on the peg in the hall, and he was once again their elderly friend. Even though he was reading, he didn't frown when Ida and Maud entered the room; he patted the sofa so they might sit beside him.

The library was the most interesting room in the house, Ida thought, and rose from prickly horsehair to see if Sir Walter Scott was still safe on the mantel. Then she went on to examine the bookcase that cheated, and was really a door . . . all of its volumes were sham, even though some of them were by Sir Walter, himself. If you pushed in just the right spot, you found yourself in a small room, quite empty, except for Auntie's cobweb-broom.

But Uncle's writing desk was better than the cheating books. On it stood the glass paper-weight that you shook to cause the toy town it enclosed to disappear in a snow-storm . . .

Then Ida saw that Mr Maufe had left the library. Maud and she had it to themselves, and they could turn somersaults on the carpet or do anything. But Mr Maufe had forgotten his book, and Maud was reading it. Ida wanted to, as well, but she only had time to see the picture of the rude lady lying on the cushion. Maud got a fright and went red and snapped the book shut. She jumped up; her cheeks were on fire.

Ida felt excited, too, so they ran out of the library like mad things, and in the garden the hollyhocks and sunflowers clashed at the sky, and the orange-flower smell was everywhere. They ran round and round and the gravel was sharp and Maud fell down but she didn't cry, even though there was blood. They trampled on Auntie's pinks but they didn't care. Then Mama was rapping on the drawing-room window, so they ran under the pines and threw themselves down in the grass. It swished and it would stain your dress and you might get an ant in your ear. Ida did once, and it had to be floated out with oil. But who cared? They were going to The Peach Groves.

PART TWO

Interlude

You were merely a child. Your viewpoint was
different to theirs. You were down low with the
table, the chair. They — the grown-ups — towered
above you. Over your head, on a level with the top
of the cabinet and the next to highest shelf, their
mouths whispered secrets. But being a child had its
advantages. You were so small that they sometimes
overlooked you: it was allowable for you to turn
anonymous. You crouched on Turkey carpet,
squeezed into the little space between the horsehair
sofa and the bookcase, and her skirts brushed
against you but she didn't know you were there. His
boots came forward to meet her. The skirt dipped
upon them, and they stood still; they were nice
boots, nigger-brown, with a high degree of polish.
Then her skirt and his boots moved out of Ida's
vision. Uncle and Tempe went into the room
behind the fake bookcase. It must be dreary in
there, with only a cobweb-broom for company.

Merely a child, Ida sensed another mystery.

59

Uncle's house was full of them: Mama loving him so much, while he, unlike all the other gentlemen, appeared to feel nothing for her . . . his strange surge of happiness after Christchurch — was it only caused by Wapiti's win?

Most mysterious of all, was Tempe. Ida was fascinated by her. It was she who, unknowing, was the cause of all that time spent crouching on library carpet and peeping from under the tent of stiff damask that fell off the dining-room table. In between social engagements, while they waited to start for The Peach Groves, whither Mr Maufe had already departed to prepare for their visit, Ida pushed time on by willing empty rooms to come to life.

For something was in the air. She was sure of it. You were a child, so small; you slipped easily in and out of the tangled patterns of the grown-ups' overlapping lives.

Ida followed Tempe to the pool again, but it wasn't so entertaining a second time — not even the part where you saw her undressed. Nor was the pine-wood nearly so fairy-tale; the strange jungle it sheltered could be dismissed as merely North Island bush. And: "Yes," Aunt Cissie mused. "I believe that somewhere nearby are the remains of an older, grander house . . ." A stone house, Auntie recalled, rare for those parts . . . but ruined now, quite crumbled away.

Tempe was more interesting when she kept her clothes on, and swept into the library and let Uncle kiss her. Then Ida was rewarded for all that time spent urging the slow minutes on and praying to God and to Queechy that a real mystery might come into being from all the little pretend ones. Uncle kissed Tempe and she didn't tell him to stop. They went into the secret room. That evening at dinner, Uncle smiled as he said grace. Mama looked pale.

Though Tempe kept her colour. Her cheeks were mottled prettily with pink, and Ida admired, and wondered if nature was aided by the rouge-pot she hid in her dressing-case.

For Ida knew Tempe's bedroom well. Often, when Tempe made her way through the needle-wood, she explored it. At first she was disappointed. The room was ordinary enough with its rose-and-ribbon wallpaper, its standard appointments.

But it was thrilling to tiptoe to the bed and lay her head on its pillow and reflect that Tempe's head rested there regularly; to admire *Shanklin Chine: Drawn in Alum Bay Sands* on the wall and fiddle with the muddle of toilet equipage on the dressing-table. Doing this, Ida reflected that, really, the room didn't seem like Tempe's at all. Everything was too dainty and insipid for her and, besides, the room resembled a museum — nothing seemed used. The beaded tidy that swung on a cord from the toilet-glass was quite empty of hair-combings; the filigree bouquet holder on the bedside table was grimy with dust.

Indeed, on closer examination, everything was in the fashion of twenty years ago. It was as if the room was full of the unknown life of someone other than Tempe.

And, just as when she had peeped into the carved chest in the hall, Ida shivered. She ran from the room and wished she had never ventured there. But went back, again and again. Somehow she couldn't help it.

Then, one day she lingered too long or Tempe decided against her dip in the pool. Ida was wondering over the delicate tints of the sand picture when she heard footsteps outside the door. Just in time, she scuttled behind the scrapwork screen. She couldn't see them but she heard their voices.

And Uncle was saying that he shouldn't be there, but Tempe was telling him that this was their chance. "Oh Harry," she said — and her voice was sugared, as if she crunched on a perfumed almond — "if you knew how I long to be with you . . ." Her voice trailed off, and Ida felt scornful, yet interested, as she listened to the series of smaller noises that meant they were spooning. Then Uncle was talking again. He said that he was worthless, but the way he said it made you feel that he enjoyed being in that state. The bed squeaked, and the small sounds that made Ida think of snails and butterflies resumed. Then from downstairs came the faint clash of the housemaid throwing knives and forks at the tablecloth. "Don't," said Tempe. "Not now." Then Uncle's boots were going out of the door; then Tempe's were doing the same.

So many new secrets were hard to keep to herself. Ida wished that she had someone to tell. Though, probably, telling someone would have made it ordinary, explainable. And, after all, there was Queechy to confide in. Of course, even as she whispered in the doll's ear, Ida knew it to be a game: Queechy was only a porcelain head atop a calico body. But precisely because she was merely a stand-in for a mortal friend, Queechy had power. You could read what you liked in her glass eyes; you were assured that her painted lips would comfort. But, somehow, all this agreeing didn't diminish her. Static, ever consoling, she was powerful. Ida couldn't do without her.

Queechy was God. Talking to her did for praying. Ida was lucky to have her when Uncle's "Worthless" turned frightening. In the dream the small moist love noises began, but instead of kisses, butterflies flew off their mouths. A slug crawled down Tempe's chin and Uncle's lips were graveyard worms. "Worthless," he said again and Ida screamed into her pillow. But Queechy made it better. Only porcelain and calico, she told Ida what to do. It turned into a joke. Queechy was more powerful than ever. Ida, never much good with her needle, kept pricking her finger, but persevered. She chose crimson thread and cross-stitch. Her WORTHLESS was a bit trembly, but the words just fitted in, across Queechy's imaginary bosom, from one of her armpits to the other.

And the nicest thing was that only the two of them knew the words were there. The doll sat propped against a cushion, simpering, and Ida felt safe. Because of Queechy and what was hidden under her petticoat, the grown-ups were diminished.

Mr Maufe dreamed, too. So often he thought of her — his little white girl. It was a comfort to have her there in the dark; she lit it with her pale dress and fall of silvery hair.

Maud was one of his choicest finds. He thought of her, and was no longer swamped by the black emptiness of night, that so often made him shiver at his anonymity as he huddled beside Wifey's snoring hulk. The sweet poppet bided her time with him over breakfast; armed him against artistic faculty and splaying thumb, and the fear almost as bad as his own in Ethel and Queenie's eyes.

He was home again but life kept on being good. Soon they would come; which really meant that soon she would be with him. Little did he think when he accepted Harry Jones's invite for Christmas that perfection would be so near to hand. There had been other pets almost as comely, on other trips to Auckland, of course, but the circumstances had always been wrong. He hated anything sordid . . . a quick fumble in the Jewish Cemetery wasn't worth much; though the time behind the Domain's lofty phoenix palm had been better.

Soon they would come to The Peach Groves — Mrs Dean and Ida and Maud. And, for luck, he'd invited Tempe, too, for it would be good to feel he had an ally. Though nothing could fail. Why should it? — nothing he did was really wrong. He was a person of breeding and taste. He possessed a genteel manner, a gentlemanly carriage; his toilette was harmonious and becoming. When he trailed the little dears he proceeded at a leisurely pace. Walking fast in the street was a mark of vulgarity, implying hurry of business; it might appear well in a mechanic or tradesman, but ill-suited a man of fashion.

He was a gentleman. Papa was acquainted with Sir George Grey, so when a certain tot turned nasty in Hyde Park and made it imperative he should speed abroad, New Zealand seemed the obvious choice. Wifey and the girls had grumbled a bit, Oc had started his habit, but soon they were settled in. They didn't have to rough it. The house had a pillared verandah; its windows were glazed with hand-spun glass. Wifey was an heiress and fear of scandal made Papa generous —he had the cash to snap up a thousand acres of grand land; the cash to ensure that others tended his flocks and herds. It was all his — the fertile pasture, the labourer's cottage, the dust-thick road — and he didn't even have to dirty his hands. He possessed the changing colours of mountains and the sound of water running over pebbles. At his command forests had been wiped out. In winter he'd watched bill-hook and axe slash through damp tangles of bracken and manuka; in autumn, taking advantage of a suitable dry spell and a favourable wind, he'd rejoiced as the match was applied. A good fire ran for miles and consumed the vegetation of ages. Mr Maufe loved a burn. The sun glowed through the haze; the ground was covered with ash: he walked through a landscape in Hell.

The land was tamed. Rye-grass and clover were sown on to the warm ashes, and before the winter there was a suspicion of thin green. As the grass grew, the forest fought back. Gingery fern fronds uncoiled, manuka seed sprouted. The new scrub had to be cut by teams of Maoris, or chewed and trodden into submission by sheep. To begin with, it was a never-ending struggle but his money won it.

Exile wasn't too bad. They'd arrived when the Maori wars were conveniently over, and the rich valleys of the Waihou were up for division. Each year civilization grew apace. Axe and fire, stock and pasture and plough all played their part. Gold was discovered near at hand — calico tents and grog shops flourished. Someone thought up a potent tipple of brandy and ginger beer: the Wellington beaches were so littered with broken bottles that it was a danger to walk there: the Woman's Christian Temperance Union gained members.

Mr Maufe was more in pocket now, than ever, since he'd mated his long-woolled Romney Marsh ewes with Southdown rams. The resulting crossbreed was ideally suited for the frozen meat trade that had flourished since '82. There were freezing works in most self-respecting towns, now; each year saw more carcasses of mutton and beef set off for England. Late spring and summer saw the young fat stock sent forward. He'd visited the slaughter-house once. He'd never forget the stench.

Once spring had meant something else. Bluebells were the colour of Holy Mary's gown, the primrose was a symbol of youth. Early days . . . Mama called him, not Augustus, but Young Apollo; she believed he was marked for a saint. He'd loved church lights and the sanctuary's fonts of pure water. His books, then, were different. He pored over the picture of the great-winged angel confronting Gideon under the oak-tree. It stood in a ray of dotted light, there was a neatly cross-hatched aspidistra at its feet.

Then, angels might be met with anywhere. He saw them, he really did; he rivalled Samuel conversing with God. Till they sent him to school —

and then he was only Maufe major. Not long after, Mama let him down worse by dying and he never forgave her.

He grew, he changed: not Young Apollo but Augustus Maufe, expelled from Eden, but with the memory of the perfect place imprinted for ever on his mind. He married Wifey early on. It was known as settling down, and Ethel was born and then Queenie and Oc. Life, he supposed, was passable, despite his nails being bitten to the quick. For he remembered; that perfect beginning plagued his mind with exquisite cruelty.

Even the books he bought furtively couldn't give him a second-hand thrill that matched the old one. And then the day came when he sighted his first poppet . . . not any little girl, this one — this one, she is mine. And it was ridiculous, but he felt he was watching himself as he used to be then. Skipping she was, just like he did . . . under the elm-tree, and his legs were slapped by the wind. She was perfect in her *broderie anglaise* . . . he'd worn skirts, too, till he was five. His favourite cap had a peak and tassel.

At first it was enough merely to look. The old contented feeling came. The dull weight rose from his mind. He could think and feel clearly, freshly.

Eventually the poppets, his gifts from God, landed him in New Zealand. Where life went on: a good day, a bad one, a worse: a spell in Auckland.

But he had to return to The Peach Groves. Where there could always be a night when he woke and was turned into nothing by the darkness; where, without doubt, there'd always be that awful half-hour before even a good night fell — that small spell of antipodean dusk when everything turned gro-

67

tesque, and the charred remnants of forests accused him; when the natural world stopped being tame and leapt free of his carefully spaced hedges of hawthorn and gorse.

Once, at dusk, he'd almost been tricked. He'd thought it was the old enchantment come back: all the scents and colours curiously heightened, a hushed stillness dominated by the great eye of the setting sun. But then he'd felt his skin prick, and was glad Wifey was cooeeing from the verandah. This time the magic held no sweetness, there was only a savage purity, something foreign and sneering.

Often the bad feeling followed him into the house; often at night he shivered. In the dark a voice spoke inside his head. *You* killed Young Apollo, it accused him. He cried then. He was only a dirty old man; a half thing with a crippled soul imprisoned in a body he loathed.

But he had a silver-topped cane and spats. He never ventured to bow to a lady upon the strength of a ballroom introduction unless she did him the honour to recognize him first. And Master Bob was coming. He could hardly bear the waiting.

They always slept with the curtains drawn back, for Ida was afraid of the dark. Sometimes Maud woke in the night. The stars were beautiful and she wanted to cry; she felt small and alone, and that was beautiful, too. Everything was, now. The cold uncaring stars, the mother-of-pearl buttons on her nightie, the moons on her fingernails. She admired her nails when she woke in the morning — they reminded her of the shells she gathered on the beach at Glenelg.

Morning, and Maud undid the mother-of-pearl buttons at her cuffs and slid back the sleeves of her night-gown. She held up her arms to the light and admired the faint blue veins, the delicate hairs. Oh, she was happy. It was a new day and the sun shone and anything might happen. One day she would have a coat with a fuzzy astrakhan collar. "One day, Master Bob . . ." and Mr Maufe bent down and whispered in her ear. She couldn't understand the words, but she dimpled, pretended. Silly old man, but nice . . . His book was, too, in another sort of way. Curious. It was best to think of something else. How "To meet, to know, to love and then to part is the sad story of many a heart" was a beauty to have in your autograph album. How Tempe said there might be a fancy ball at The Peach Groves . . . Dreamily, Maud went on stroking her arms, till Ida stirred and she had to stop. She could never enjoy things with Ida's eyes watching. Ida saw — she remembered; she wasn't like other people's sisters. And always escorted by that ridiculous doll.

She had even chosen to bring it the day Tempe took them to the top of Mount Eden. A queer day, that, and an ancient volcanic cone was disappointing. What, from your window, appeared mysteriously other-worldly was, on closer inspection, merely a favourite Sunday resort: a grassy slope thickly populated with picnickers, lying on their backs in the sun or discreetly flirting in a pine-tree's shade . . . On and on they'd trudged to the summit. Ida carried Queechy, Maud the billy packed with sandwiches, Tempe the bottle of cold tea. The sun burned through their hats, and Tempe kept imparting useless facts. Who cared that they climbed a Maori fortress; that *here* were once trenches and look-out towers; *there*, pits where the season's food was stored? Tempe was peculiar. Some of the family parties stared. She had twined a wreath of leaves round the crown of her hat, and her hair had come loose to cloud her face. All the time she talked loudly of a mountain unrelated to the hill they climbed.

At last they had reached the summit, and then it was better. They had a wonderful view of Auckland and the harbour; the crater was as good as the Whispering Gallery in the dome of St Paul's in London. They tried it out with their names. *Ida, Ida . . . Maud, Maud . . .* the crater dutifully amplified back. But Tempe didn't bother to give it a try. Now they had got to the top she seemed to have lost interest in the excursion. She slumped down and chewed at a stalk of five-finger, and didn't worry that her skirt might get stained with green. Maud set the bottle of cold tea upright and felt virtuous. Ida went on calling; the crater answered her sadly.

Tempe was queer. Maud lay in bed and thought of her. She wasn't someone you could neatly label, and go on to dismiss comfortably. Maud sighed and hoped she wasn't starting a headache. She didn't like Tempe and it was a nuisance — usually she liked nearly everyone, and never gave them a thought. Somehow Tempe wasn't ladylike. She made you feel that all the nice things — Princess Beatrice's wedding to dashing Prince Henry of

Battenberg, Mama's moss-rose tea-set — didn't mean much at all.

But poor Tempe was an orphan, and Auntie wasn't sympathetic, and how dull to be a brunette... The curtains flapped at the window and beyond them the sky was blue. It would be a lovely day, Maud was sure. She would practise "Twickenham Ferry" for The Peach Groves. If there was a fancy ball, the Roses of York and Lancaster was a suitable costume for sisters. Mama would make a perfect Arctic Maiden.

※

In those days flounces and frills weren't hemmed, but used to be pinked at the edges by special little machines found at the shops of undertakers, who used them on shrouds and the linings of coffins. It was one of her greatest pleasures to take trimmings to such places. The sound of hammering coffins, mingled with the noise of the pinking machine, interested her greatly.

Was that true? Was Death so close even then, as she waited for the flounces for her party dress? Strange — she hardly believed some of the things that came into her head... the flounces and Zillah Whiffin waiting patiently, enjoying the hammering. Poor Zillah, she was remarkably plain. So much so, that Augustus's pet name for her was the Boiled Bull-dog. It wasn't exactly marriage by fascination, but the Whiffin inheritance compensated for much: they were wed at Kensington Old Church one June.

And, at first, marriage meant living in a dream.

She was a sleep-walker who smiled placidly through the pleasant round of her days. Life was a little affair of dinner parties and dances, pagoda sleeves and Paisley shawls. Augustus had his quiet spells, but she supposed it to be wedded bliss. The girls were born, and for a while she stopped dreaming: the pain was terrible but she liked it — for once she was doing something real. But the realness never lasted. Baby always came back tidied up; there was a wet-nurse. Most days you lay a lot on the drawing-room sofa; sometimes you were surprised by the sound of crying from upstairs. Was there really a child in the house?

To start with, Oc tricked her. "It's a bonny little lad, sound wind and limb," said Doctor and she was disappointed. He took his gruel and physic so nicely and sucked at Nursie's breast so hard that she was as frightened of him as of Ethel and Queenie. But then Baby started being restless. He cried constantly and no amount of soothing syrup would make him stop. One day Wifey left her sofa to inspect him. He'd turned scrawny; it seemed true that he was really hers.

He was a sickly creature. He had a small lolling head and match-stick limbs, and was always taking colds and coughs. But Wifey was happy in winter; its coming meant she could love him more. In winter, Oc wore one of her stockings to bed, wound round his dear sore throat. Winter was castor-oil time; was when Oc sat on her lap before the fire, while she warmed the piece of brown paper and rubbed it with a Russian tallow candle and wrapped it round his sweet little chest. She always remembered the strange smell of the plaster —

penetrating and aromatic. Why couldn't he stay a child for ever?

When he went away to school she had her attack. The moon was a toenail cutting in the sky: she laughed and laughed, it was so funny. She put her nose up close to the window and the moon came closer — not a toenail paring now, but swollen, swelling: a fiery pearl, perhaps, though misty at the edges, as if the moon was wrapped in gauze. There were birds in the sky, too — great black birds; she must be careful or they might peck her nose. The leaves on the drawing-room carpet swirled uneasily. *Zillah, Zillah*, she heard the leaves whisper, *you must take care.* The moon was bright and the birds kept up a terrible piping. *Beware, beware* warned the carpet, and she ripped at her collar, she tore her dress so her chest could get free.

Augustus said she must rise. She was a big woman, heavy, but he lifted her off the carpet; he put her on the sofa and covered her up — it was shameful that he should find her like that. "You are ill, Wifey," he said and the moon moved back. Doctor came to hold her hand and purse his lips. "Dreams to the dreamer are realities," he said. They dosed her with ipecacuanha powder to make her vomit; they cut her hair short so that her brain might keep cool. It was fever with delirium, Doctor said, and Nurse crept about in list slippers. One day she fell into a long sleep which lasted thirty-seven hours. It was the turning-point of the disease, and she woke with her mind restored, and from that time commenced a new life.

Now Wifey was a visionary artist. Straight away, on waking, she felt she had an artistic faculty seeking expression. It took various forms. First came the knitting: the wool, different coloured, looping through your fingers and you trembled with excitement at what might appear . . . sometimes it was an old man's beard she made — it rippled in waves and waterfalls, and the old man's dewlaps hid behind it. The inspirational writings came next. She wrote very small; it was like being the man who fitted in the Lord's Prayer in pin-pricks on the sea-shell. The words were strange, like the ones in Revelations. Wifey wrote of black suns and bloody moons, of a sea of glass and a coral hill. The writing frightened her. She fell down on the carpet again, and they sent her to the forest to recover. The trees muttered and creaked; their leaves rustled and twittered constantly. Wifey felt comforted as she walked beneath them. Her head came clear and she went back to London and started tearing up clothes. For now the faculty must be served with needle and thread, and for appliqué you needed a sufficiency of scraps.

Queenie's Garibaldi bodice provided a lovely red; Ethel's Zouave jacket the perfect blue. Augustus, pleased to see her occupied, got in a roll of canvas. She stitched at a picture of a happy family: Mama and baby Oc. An older Oc came home with the good conduct medal from school, but she didn't have much to say to him. His small head had grown so large that she hardly knew him. They nodded when they passed in the passage and made conversation politely at table. But the real Octavius was captured by the tip of her flying needle; held in place with herring-bone stitch and French knots.

The day before she completed her fourth canvas, Augustus said Doctor advised a long sea voyage. Wifey concentrated on threading her needle and nodded. Yes, New Zealand would make a change, but where was it? More important, did he think the new spangled wools too gay in appearance, should she have stuck to her trusty crystal twines?

They had a pleasant voyage, it was said by those who understood sea voyages, but she did not like it much. The waves were thrilling but she was not moved to stitch. She could not eat the biscuits — she was nearly starved, though some people grew quite fat and said they had never lived so well in their lives. But there was always something to entertain you. One day Queenie lost two hats overboard and Oc's flannel waistcoat was blown off the clothes-line. And twelve people died, most of them children. But oh dear, what if the artistic faculty had not chosen to accompany her to foreign parts?

Wifey needn't have worried, for New Zealand wasn't so strange. Soon the new house had Nottingham lace curtains and several housemaids whose print skirts crackled reassuringly with starch. Night wasn't so antipodean when it was lit with the small moons of familiar lamp globes. You ate dinner off your usual Rockingham plate.

It was the other side of the world, but in no time at all the lilacs came out and Queenie stood under the hawthorn-tree and sighed for Fred who wrote regularly from India.

Life was good. The faculty hadn't proved faithless: now Wifey practised inspired piano playing. She sat at the pianoforte, pedalling vigorously; while her hands wandered over the keyboard she shut her eyes and ignored the racket and sang a hymn she remembered from childhood:

Oh, wash me Lord, I pray Thee,
That so my soul may grow
As pure as is the lily,
And whiter than the snow.

In the new land she came out of herself a bit. She seemed like a standard mama as she complimented Oc on his latest fly-leaf, and worried over Ethel's lack of admirers, and brushed the hawthorn petals from Queenie's hair.

But Queenie's young man died. Wifey stopped playing the piano to start drawing in pen and ink.

It was an odd sort of faculty that possessed her, now — not so pleasurable, almost a torment. Augustus frowned and said she had always been too intense; he suggested a turn about the garden. Wifey shook her head and stayed put. Augustus didn't understand. He would have sneered if she'd told him of her guide.

In the past she had longed for a companion sympathetic to her creating. So when she first sensed the spirit's presence she was overjoyed; at first, drawing was fun.

But soon she had her doubts. Wifey's spirit guide allowed her no rest; she felt guilty when she wasn't bent over her sketch-block, in the box-room that served as a studio. And the nuisance took delight in teasing — he talked continually about death, even as he urged on her pen. Death was waiting to pounce, he warned. *Take care*, he urged, just as the leaves on the carpet had, long ago. She nodded, she had always known . . . even as she masqueraded as the child Zillah, listening to hammers falling on

76

coffins as her party frills were pinked. Death wasn't anything much, she told him; at times it was very welcome. Her spirit guide seemed disappointed that she kept so composed. He told her sternly that she had a task . . . there was much to accomplish before she could allowably depart. Death could be tricky. Mistakes might be made; you could be summoned before your time.

After that it was awful. Wifey's pen must move faster than ever. At times the activity kept her from sleeping — she worked through the night at feverish speed, filling up the drawing-books Augustus brought her from Auckland. The pictures didn't always please her; often they were merely scribbles. But she wasn't responsible; she hid the drawing-books in her travelling trunk.

And she took care. Eyes were important, so she drank carrot juice with every meal, and did exercises with a pencil, and wore a green eye-shade. She kept the blinds in the box-room pulled down. With a spirit guide at your fingertips it was easy to draw in the dark.

⁂

Tempe had wanted to reach the mountain for so long. It was a symbol, one of the touchstones of her private world. Each morning she woke and saw it — only a little way distant, looming close. Yet it wasn't *too* near. The journeying stayed something you looked forward to; that little distance guaranteed mystery. The mountain remained as meaningful as the secret pool and the forest walk towards it. It was as much Tempe's as the room in

Cissie's house that was dedicated to Linda. Because of those few miles between them, the mountain had all the potency of myth.

It had stayed her mountain, even when Cissie announced proudly that her rockery was built of Mount Eden scoria; even when Mr Maufe brought her the history book from town. This book was old; it told her things she wanted to know: not Mount Eden but Maungawhau, not merely Tempe's mountain but other people's, too . . . She read and read, and learned things to tell Ida and Maud. Though why it had been necessary that the children should accompany her to the summit, wasn't easy to say. It was a surprise when she'd heard her voice ask them to come. It was queer, because that day she hated them worse than usual; that day when Harry came to her in the room behind the bookcase he seemed to be thinking of Blanche Dean. If he was, Harry was silly, for Tempe could easily take her revenge. Maud was the image of her mama; she'd do perfectly for that wax dolly you pricked with pins. If Harry's eyes kept playing traitor something horrid would happen to Miss Maud. It would be easy, for they were going to The Peach Groves, where Mr Maufe waited to play host. Strange, though, how hating them, Tempe had suggested a picnic. She wondered why, and concluded the most likely reason to be that it was somehow important she should show them her power.

But it wasn't her mountain when she got there. This mountain was only a hill; this hill was dotted with people. It was all right to share Maungawhau with those mentioned in Mr Maufe's book (they were Linda's people and thus poetic: the widows

78

were crowned with seaweed chaplets, the warriors wore greenstone ear-rings), but the picnic parties on Mount Eden bore the book-people no relation. It was Cissie's tribe that spread luncheon cloths, and trod Mount Eden in Sunday shoes. It was unbelievable that their niceness and smallness, their hair-pins and three-button gloves had the strength to cancel out her dreaming. No more land of the long white cloud. No more Earth Mother and Sky Father and Great Girl of Night. There is no woman in the moon, no spider's web stretching to heaven.

Tempe shuddered and hugged the bottle of cold tea closer, and wanted to cry — even more so when they reached the summit. For the crater made you think of an egg-cup and the juveniles, when they weren't testing its echo, lit fires to emulate eruption. Ingenious Aucklanders spoke of cementing its insides, so the crater might serve the purpose of a reservoir.

The mountain had turned benign; it had forgotten its fiery beginnings. It wouldn't resist as all about it the little houses sprang up, as the bridle-paths and country lanes became roads. Already, the land was tamed. Bells tinkled amongst the fern, signifying that cattle grazed there. Old districts were wiped out; old names disregarded. The Very Rev. Comrie stated in *The Presbytery of Auckland* that *Whau* meant Wilderness, which was unattractive in meaning: soon you lived at Avondale, not Whau . . . And: "Auckland is swarming with them," said Cissie, "even to a greater extent than usual." It was shocking, she said, how every door-step in Upper Queen Street had a group sitting on it. A visit to town wasn't a pleasure any more. You just saw big

Maoris, little Maoris, old Maoris, young Maoris. Squatting about on the door-steps, looking decidedly uncivilized with their pipes and tattooed chins . . . And Tempe had reached the mountain at last. She sat on the summit of Mount Eden and knew that everything was ruined, and wondered if it had happened because of what she'd done . . . For: "These ones are poison," said Mother. "You must be careful of these," and she jerked the flax basket away. She meant that karaka kernels and tutu berries were as bad as the katipo spider's bite . . . I must be careful, thought Tempe, as she measured out just enough. But it was easy — easier than she'd imagined, to slip a little into Cissie's wineberry jelly.

Tempe poisoned Cissie to punish Harry, who had said that loving Tempe was wrong. "It should never have happened," he said and he meant the evening when their dallying under the pine-trees stopped being innocent; when he loved her and she forgot Linda and the mountain and everything else, even the fact that she was Cissie's sister and he was Cissie's husband. It worried him, though, and one evening he started crying. She felt like Harry's mama as he buried his head in her lap and confided. He said it was a relief to tell someone at last. How he was worthless and not just because of Tempe (whom he would never touch again), but also because of Blanche. "I love her so much," he said and at first Tempe didn't know what he meant. When she understood, she hated Blanche Dean for having him first. After that, for a while, Harry and Tempe played at strangers and Cissie took sick. Doctor couldn't think up a cure. There was no one to tell him that for karaka kernels and tutu berries the sufferer should be buried to the neck in earth, or immersed in water, or suspended over a slowly smoking fire.

Cissie recovered, and Blanche Dean arrived, and Harry loved Tempe again. But Tempe would never forget how her body had been so lonely — and not for Mother or the pool or the mountain; how, lying in bed, wishing Harry would come to her, she had scorned her body as it betrayed the sacred things. You could do worse than deceive Cissie or pick karaka berries. On those nights she had wanted Harry so much that she would have done anything to make him come to her — even turned the Tempe who was wild and scorning of *their* world into a Tempe who conformed and promenaded on Mount Eden, stabbing the soft mountain turf with the ferrule of her pagoda parasol and her fashionable Louis heels.

***

Home. It is a lofty fantasy, a folly. There are towers and turrets and gables. There is much fret-sawn wood and terra-cotta frilling and spider-webs like lacy Valentines. Locally, it is known as the Calendar House, because it has three hundred and sixty-five windows to represent the days of the year, fifty-two rooms (the weeks of the year), twelve chimneys (the months), seven entrances (the days of the week), and four staircases (the seasons).

There is an entrance hall, and the fishing-rod rack holds a collection of walking-sticks made from woods of the district. The mounted heads on the wall are Japanese deer and wild Kerry goat. The antlers over the mantelpiece are those of a giant Irish elk, extinct for over ten thousand years. An oak whip-rack holds one coachman's whip. There is a Map Room and a Blue Room as well as everything else, but somehow the hall is usually as far as you get. Outside is more interesting.

There, Home is a secret. It is half-hidden by a curtain of trembling ivy. There are birds' nests in the ivy — you will let the birds be ravens. And there is a garden: fat roses, of course, always losing their petals; more ivy, always shiny with rain. There are rustling leaves and paths that are mostly moss. There is a waterfall and a river you must cross on a little rope-bridge. Though, sometimes, you paddle towards the rapids in your Indian canoe. Snakes doze in neatly arranged coils or slip past your ankles through the ferns. Wolves snap their teeth, but you press closer. Behind you the three hundred and sixty-five windows glow with light, where they are not covered with ivy. There is a vast solitude and darkness is falling, but you determine to reach her. This time she is guarded by a dragon with nine heads. You will dash forward with your sword and kill the dragon. She will open her eyes and give you a ring and half of her handkerchief. She will not call you little monster, and say that you ought to be put in the circus...

But that was as far as imagining took him. The princess opened her eyes, but he could never think of what came next. There wasn't any happy ending, the story petered out, and he knew that none of it was true. The Calendar House was in Tasmania and the rapids in the *Boy's Own Annual*. He wasn't Prince Charming, but only Oc Maufe, whose head was so large that at school he'd been popularly known as Melon.

Poor Oc. Dreaming was never enough; hard facts constantly intruded. Reality was other people — their mouths spilling the sharp words that hurt him, their eyes so cold that he felt muddled and more clumsy than ever. "Octavius is doing it again, Nursie," the little girls cried behind Mama's back, and he wasn't allowed to suck his thumb. Now he didn't suck, but sort of thumped it, and they called it his habit and said it was nerves, and because he was grown-up they let him do it. But their eyes — judging, scorning — reduced the comfort of thumbing considerably. Queenie and Ethel had the knack of ruining things. It was their fault that his imagining must always keep outdoors. He saw the outside of Home perfectly — the turrets, the towers, the gables — but he could never get past the hall.

Once they had been little girls with sashes and coral necklaces; so pretty, that Oc was sure that, grown, Ethel's looks would rival those of the goose-girl who was really a princess and Queenie would outshine Cherry, before she became frog-bride. It was a surprise, then, to see them turn into quite something else. Sometimes he wondered if it was really Ethel — this pale lady, with a miserable expression, and undergarments of natural undyed sanitary wool, who spent most of each day fretting that the Editor of the *G.O.P.* should find her latest poetical effort incorrect in metre. And was this Queenie — this other lady (just as miserable, not so pale), who *felt* her poetry rather than gave it utterance (which meant she was usually all of a tremble or on the verge of a swoon because of being passionately fond of scenery, flowers, sunsets, moonlight, autumnal tints and spring perfume)?

Octavius, though — he resembled a prince, so handsome and with such beautiful eyes that when the princess awoke she gave her consent and they set out full of joy for the prince's kingdom, where they lived happily a great many years. Not true, though. Oc had the watermelon head, and was small and didn't know what to do with his hands. "Stop thumbing, laddy," Mama said absently, rapping his knuckles fondly. That was in the beginning, when they had first come to The Peach Groves. Mama was ordinary, almost, then. She took an interest in his books, he had someone to talk to. Really, it seemed that he hadn't talked for years. He was scared of Queenie and Ethel and Papa, and so he mostly kept quiet. But now Mama was herself, and she'd bang down the piano lid, which meant that her inspiration was over for the day; they'd settle in the drawing-room before the tea-tray and he could confide.

Oc improved, and didn't waggle his thumb so much, but when the piano lid stayed permanently shut and she began drawing, his habit took a turn for the worse. He stopped talking; he only had his hobby. And, because of it, Papa started being his friend. He came back from Auckland and brought up his books. He had to stoop because the ceiling of Oc's work-room in the attic was low, but he didn't complain, even though he had cobwebs on his frock-coat. Next door in the box-room, Mama's pen was scratching in the dark; now she evaded him, there were no more toast- and tea-times, but here was Papa asking his advice, saying: "Can anything be done with this one, dear boy? . . . Can you match this binding?"

Suddenly the work-room was a cosy place. Papa and he were men together. Of course he could mend them, he said, and Papa patted his shoulder and warned sternly: "Don't strain your eyes over any of the small print, Octavius. Do you promise you won't read a word?"

Oc hummed as he worked, sometimes into the night. His shadow kept him company on the wall as the oil lamp glowed and he hunched over the sewing-frame and his hand sped with the needle. He was happy. It didn't matter that Mama ignored him and that Home didn't exist. This was real: Octavius Maufe lived at The Peach Groves and would never be King of the Golden Mountain, but Papa patted his shoulder and said: "Perfect, dear boy," when he came to collect his books. He reckoned Oc had done his mending well, so there'd certainly be a next time, and there was, and another one after that. And this time there were some terrors to sew, with most of the pages come loose; this time there were pictures.

Well, looking at the pictures wasn't reading. And the first one wasn't too bad — it was probably a mistake . . . Queenie and Ethel weren't like that — were they? Oh dear. Oc started to sweat, he felt dizzy. It was shameful, but he couldn't stop looking. His mind went astray, and his thoughts ran hither and thither like so many wild animals, and the pictures got worse. He felt burning inside, then cold. Then he felt terrible: low, lonely — he felt afraid. The work-room wasn't cosy any more, and he shivered and his thumb was sore, for all the time he'd been doing his habit. That was a comfort — he had that. And he had the goose-girl and Snow-drop who slept in a coffin of glass. That world wasn't dirty: the towers, the ivy, the fifty-two rooms; snakes dozing, rope-bridges, wolves snapping . . .

Life went on. Oc kept sewing for Papa, and didn't look once. Ethel used her dumb-bells ten minutes before breakfast and went on pondering metre. Queenie continued being a lover of Nature, and felt a joy akin to rapture when she stood on the summit of some lofty hill, etcetera. But wasn't it queer how, after a good ramble, she always enjoyed a spell in the kitchen playing Cook, and then that night there was always lamb's head for dinner. Funny. She pushed up her Liberty silk sleeves and worked neatly and carefully . . . take the head with neck attached, split up the forehead and take out the brains and lay aside. Wash the head, take out the eyes, clean out the nose with salt . . . Her hands were bathed in blood, and she always thought of Fred in India — how did he die? — and perhaps his head had been split in halves; cracked and separated, for all the world like a walnut. There was the grey brain interspersed with thin streaks of blood. Oh, gentle Jesus — the terrible images, she couldn't pray them away. There were no hawthorn petals in Queenie's hair now, but her eyes shone so prettily, her face was flushed and her lips curled back in a queer little smile. She looked sort of triumphant, the real Cook thought. She was a demon for work, Miss Queenie — all the time her hands kept moving . . . rub it over with an egg well beaten, strew crumbs of bread, pepper and salt . . . Lamb's head always tasted delicious when Queenie cooked it.

Now he was Major Jones, husband of Cissie, who lived at Epsom where the volcanic soil was choice, who raced Wapiti and Nelson, and moved amongst the élite of Auckland. But *then* he'd been merely second son, and Pa was a bloody great bully, and Major Jones never forgot. How they called it home, but you slept like sardines, with three at the top and two at the bottom; and tea was always pigs' tails and marrow bones. You knew you were meant for better things and Bets was the only one who understood. Bets was a little lady despite the dirt: perhaps she would do for a parlour-maid, though the embroidery factory was more likely.

Harry always won in the spelling-bee, but Pa took him away from school, and first there was the fur trade, but the bag of wadding was heavy and the dye stank like Hell. Pa whacked him because not working meant a stigma instead of pennies, and next was the shoe factory and pulling the barrow at the wood turner's; then he started at the veg stall. But the lifting was too much, with the taters in hundredweight bags, so Harry said Sod this and took the excursion train to the country. Bets came, too — she'd washed her face and turned into a stranger. You'd never meet a better girl than Bets and why should some street rough, someone like Pa, get her? The buttercups were out, and they were the only ones around for miles.

There was a girl had a baby by her brother, and that was a terrible thing, but nothing happened to Bets. She only got older and started at the factory. Harry was doing painting and glazing now, and sent off for the self-instruction book for the banjo, but more often he thought of sailing overseas — trying another land, turning into a different person. One day Pa walloped him worse than usual and that did it. Mam was scared of the workhouse, and saved pennies in a lustre ware tea-pot. Though she was better than Pa, Harry didn't like her much. He didn't feel guilty as the money went into his pocket. Bets came to London, too. The Emigrants' Information Office was at Westminster.

There was only riff-raff for company on the voyage, but they started practising accents early on, and by the time they reached South Australia they were a better class of person.

In Adelaide, Harry prospered — mostly by following the gee-gees, but also by peddling patent medicines. Professor Jones's Pile Cure did well, likewise his Amorette Nerve Tonic, but the Baby Friend Opiate let him down. It sold all right, but the mothers started complaining, for this tot and that seemed in danger of staying under permanently. It was homeopathy, and Harry even had a diploma printed to prove it, but the boys in blue weren't satisfied. They had the cheek to call Harry a pest of society, they even mentioned fraud. So he had to kiss Bets goodbye. It was sensible to leave before they laid charges, and New Zealand was really quite near.

But though they called it God's Own Country, the land of perpetual summer, that winter it rained a lot up north. And the landscape wasn't anything to write home about. Northland to Harry was a gum-field: Northland was a monotonous waste. What trees there were, were dwarfed to the level of tea-tree and fern. The soil had spent itself ages ago, producing a forest of kauri. The Maoris had treated the great trees with respect, cutting them down circumspectly, after ceremonies to appease the forest gods. Civilized man didn't bother with such niceties, but cut blindly, unmercifully. Now the only trace of kauri in Harry's Northland was the hardened sap which nested in the soil as nuggets of amber gum.

Gum could change your life. It was easier in the past, of course — once you could make your fortune just by picking bits up. But the days of easy pickings were over — now Harry had to use a probing spear and a spade. Still, these were the palmy days of digging and, if you applied yourself, money might be easily made.

Life was simple. Once you'd staked out a claim, no one could work your ground. The only tools needed were the spear, the spade and a sack. At night in your hut of sacks and mud and tea-tree you scraped the dirt from your finds. Your market was the nearest store.

It was a queer life, out on the gum-field. For weeks, perhaps, Harry wouldn't see a soul. If he did, it was only at a distance, for the diggers liked to keep to themselves. It was this freedom that attracted the adventurers who made the fields famous. Your neighbour, digging at a distance, might be a pastry-cook, a professor, or the son of an earl.

Some men couldn't stand the melancholy. In winter the stink of mud and stagnant water could get you down. And there were the swamp rats, and the fear that your luck had changed; that you would end as a skeleton in the fern, or die of pneumonia in a leaky hut. With some, the loneliness took its toll, and if suicide didn't tempt you there was always the public house next to the gum-store.

But Harry was happy on the gum-field. After a while the bareness of the landscape soothed his eye; he didn't even care when it rained. The aloneness was the hardest thing at first, but after a while that was what he liked best. Alone, Harry felt himself to be that other person he'd always dreamed of; alone, Harry found God.

In England, God had merely been an eye in the sky in Granma's greasy little book of devotions. God was Papa to Jesus who died a horrid death on the cross. In England you didn't feel safe, because you looked in Granma's other book — the big fat green one with the gold edge to every page — and it had a picture of Jesus hanging crucified, and the nails might have pierced you, not Him (you felt them going in, the picture was that real). But, feeling, you couldn't stop turning pages. Peter's cross was upside down, and Andrew's was shaped like an X . . . the stories at the back of Granma's *Life of Christ*, about what happened to the Holy Apostles and Evangelists, got worse. If that was God, you didn't want Him. Besides, Sunday was the day you hated most. On Sundays, Mam said Pa wasn't to drink; on Sundays he walloped you more. And the church bells rang, to remind you of being only scum. Sundays weren't meant for Harry Jones and his like.

Well, Harry and Bets were intimate down among the buttercups and the grown-up Harry knew that he was damned. Which was why it didn't matter what he did. Gambling was all right for scum, ditto the homeopathic cures. But north of Auckland, in the aloneness of the gum-fields, another God was revealed. This One started off by being just the wind in Harry's hair. It felt nice, and Harry sat down in the fern and shut his eyes. Then the feeling spread all over Harry's body — it was a warm, contented feeling; Harry had never felt so peaceful. But he had to go on digging, because he was on the gum-field to make his fortune, so he jumped up and the feeling left him, and he didn't give it another thought. But the next day and the next, even though there wasn't a wind, the peaceful feeling was in his hair and swooping down inside him. The wind wasn't blowing — it was only imagination, Harry knew; it wasn't something you gave a second thought to — really, it was unimportant . . . but he felt happy, he worked harder than ever, and in no time at all his sack was full of gum. Then one day, digging, he realized that the feeling had been with him for ages. And then it seemed it never left him, and he called the feeling God.

The nicest thing was, that the feeling — named — kept on being delicate, intangible. Harry's God was considerate and didn't bother him with the banalities of prophetic voices, or offer sticky-beak advice. You didn't have to spit on your finger and leaf through the Scriptures or brush up your Sunday suit; you weren't obliged to chit-chat with fellow travellers. Harry stayed alone: aloneness was Harry and God, and for the first time Harry felt a proper man. The past was finally wiped out. This God wasn't Granma's, but his own; he wasn't served with crosses or mealy-mouth Jesus. Instead, He seemed something to do with the great sweep of empty sky over Harry's head, and the swamp rat scurrying through the reeds, and the swamp hen rising with a flutter from the rapou.

And Harry wondered what would happen when he left the gum-field and stopped being alone — for you had to stock up on supplies, you had to take your gum to the store. But he did these things, and still felt at peace.

It was always good to be back. He spent his evenings sorting the day's diggings, and sometimes as he scraped and cleaned he thought of Bets — but calmly, fondly, for it was someone else who'd lain with her in the meadow. Bets loved pretty things . . . Harry began putting aside pieces of gum that he thought might please her. There was a big piece he polished carefully, until it was as clear as amber glass. There were other pieces — some streaked with reddish-brown, others clouded with inky-black. One piece had a spider embedded in its centre; another, honey-coloured, he carved into a heart — and then heated a pin and stuck it in, and deftly turned a loop: now all that was needed was a ribbon, and Bets could wear the heart round her throat.

But when he visited her at Glenelg things went wrong. Harry's God deserted him: the peaceful feeling disappeared. Confronting a fleshly Bets (who was now more properly Blanche, who belonged to George), not merely a memory, Harry didn't feel calm.

Blanche made him turn into the old Harry. They went to the races and he smoked a cigar and he wanted her all over again. He played at Uncle and pinched Maud's cheek, swung Ida high in the air, but when George was at the Law Society dinner, Blanche came into his room.

But the peace came back when he returned to the gum-field, and it was all right writing to her once a week and he thought: I love her, but I will never see her again. He kept on digging until he had enough money to turn into a gentleman — so much money that he could keep on feeling good: he didn't have to take the sort of job that would work God away. He bought new clothes and went to Wellington for a holiday, and down there he met Cissie. Confronted by all her respectability, on an impulse, he added the "Major". It worked like a charm, and they were married. She wasn't much to look at, but somehow her sharpness held him, it wasn't only the money. He admired her spirit; though she spoke badly to the servants she appreciated a good thoroughbred.

Harry gained Wapiti and Nelson and the house at Epsom, but after a while he lost the feeling of peace. Sometimes he thought of it wistfully.

And then Cissie's papa died and Tempe came to live with them. And it was like being close to Blanche all over again. Harry couldn't help himself. The guilt afterwards was terrible, for what he felt was guilt compounded. Harry felt judged for losing that perfect peace he'd known on the gum-field, as much as for what he'd done with Blanche and what he did with Tempe.

***

Cissie knew how they saw her — a little woman, scrawny, with a screwed-up face and a voice like a cockatoo. She knew, also, what they said; sometimes when it was a bad day she heard their voices clearly:

"She is frightfully delicate. There is always something internal, always a mustard poultice" ... "She makes herself ill by all that fussing about. She never does any sewing and seldom reads, so the consequence is she is eternally rushing after either Cook or Housemaid — neither of whom thank her for the trouble" ... "She reminds me of Mrs Candour in *School for Scandal.* People's characters are mown down like grass before her, and cast into the fire."

She didn't see a joke quickly. And no one seemed really fond of her; indeed, it would be a relief to give her a good shaking. For she was exacting and jealous and hysterical and prudish and backbiting and lackadaisical and ever so much more.

All her life she had been aware of *them* and their judgment. Obediently, she had lived up to her lack of looks, and acted out the part assigned to her. It was odd how, all through the years, there'd been that conveniently conventional ugly-duckling part for her to fill. Cissie was little-girl-lost crying behind the curtain because Mother didn't want her. Cissie was the plainest girl at the Academy — the blue-stocking who didn't appear grateful for an ornamental education, but must constantly have her nose in a book; who lifted that decidedly *retroussé* organ only to conceive a hopeless passion for the drawing master who, just as conventionally, scorned her. Then Cissie: sitting out "The Lily-of-the-valley Waltz" behind a potted palm; dutifully shedding crocodile tears while Mother coughed away that last illness.

Death unexpectedly excited Cissie. Its insolence was thrilling. Mother had been snatched away against her will; though she fought by clutching at the sheets and hoarding the coughs that weakened her, she hadn't a chance of winning. *They* weren't invincible, after all. Fancy, that Mother had died when a new ballgown hung in her closet, when the milliner was making her a Tyrolese hat of black silk.

But then Father started dancing. Linda drifted on his arm across the ballroom and he took her home and put her into his bed. Cissie pebble-painted on and knew she was trapped. Now *they* meant Linda. When Tempe was born, she was *them*, too.

It was easy to hate when a fairy-tale world was so close, when your own world was bitter and crabbed. Yet when Linda died, Cissie didn't rejoice as much as she might have, for by then she'd met Harry.

When Cissie put off her mourning, the last reminder of Linda went, too. Tempe hardly seemed real and, for the first time she could recall, Cissie felt free. The familiar pattern of failure seemed broken. She was still plain, but Harry appeared to prefer her like that. She supposed him to be a sort of Puritan. Any standard display of female beauty caused him to wince.

At first, being married was blissful; Cissie's voice grew sharper. She had even started to read again, had started some time before the ceremony. The books came from Sydney in a sober brown wrapping. She shuddered a little to begin with, but then she couldn't stop reading, for *The Wife's Handbook* was as thrilling as Death. Cissie learned interesting things. That the mouth of a blind puppy served better than a nipple glass in emptying the breasts of their content in case of milk fever. That Dr Tilt recommended that a wet-nurse's hair be brown and dark rather than flaxen or red because, in the former, the milk was rich in nutrient value and she was less liable to inflammation of the breast. Each evening at bedtime Cissie read a bit more. Now she'd left bosoms behind, and was up to the *sanctum sanctorum*. Her cheeks flushed pink as she savoured the interesting words: *sponge, douche, diaphragm, night-cap*. The last she felt to be her favourite, for the word conjured up a series of images that made her more than a little excited ... then drowsy, drowsier ... with *night-cap* Cissie always slept sound.

But by day, particularly when Harry sat beside her on the sofa taking tea, the images seemed nothing to do with them. How could marriage license them to lie together in a big bed like that, with no interference necessary to the usual course of proceedings until the last few moments of bliss? How could that be Harry, his satisfaction about to be completed by the stupendous effort of the vital stream, warning the lady (Cissie) who, previous to yielding herself to his arms, had softened a night-cap in warm water? And — taking tea, recalling last night's fancies — Cissie's fingers trembled so much that she nearly dropped her cup. Surely those other fingers could never be Cissie's, too? — snatching the horrid thing from under her pillow and, with thumbs and forefingers, drawing it over the burning machine (Harry's), which might then be instantly replaced in its natural receptacle for the fruition of mutual love, the entire interruption not occupying more than five or six seconds.

The Wife's Handbook said connection was natural, that without it a lady began to droop. Cissie supposed she'd weather through; she'd have to, for a wife's noblest function was her goal. She who rocked the cradle ruled the world: Cissie conned motherhood with awe. Birth presented a dizzily dangerous prospect. You lay on your left side with legs drawn up, yet at the same time you walked a razor's edge. Morning sickness and peculiar longings, fainting fits and the whites behind you, miscarriage successfully skirted, you teetered on for your prize — came closer than ever before to friend Death. Oh yes, Harry could do anything he pleased if the end result was that ultimate confrontation that Cissie knew she'd win for sure.

But all that eye strain over the handbook's pages was wasted, and all those anticipatory balancing acts led Cissie nowhere. Marriage, once the honeymoon state of bliss wore off and the house at Epsom ceased being a novelty, meant a funny state of affairs. For, married, Harry hardly touched her. There'd been a dutiful coming together on their wedding night, a half-hearted jab, a small spilling of blood. Cissie supposed it to have been defloration, and occasionally Harry did it again, and for a little while after she counted the days. But her body always let her down; then Harry did, too. For a long time, now, they'd lived together like brother and sister.

It was sad, of course, that the layette of health-preserving flannel she'd stitched so hopefully didn't have a use; but the worst thing was that, married, Cissie wasn't sure who she was. Always, before, there'd been a set part she'd known how to play.

Cissie had been faultless as Academy blue-stocking, then jealous stepdaughter and old-maid elect. All those years before Harry came she'd been perfectly unhappy, but at least she was someone, easily definable, comforted by the knowledge that count-less others had lived out similar ugly-duckling rôles before her.

Beyond that happy-ever-after cutting off of the past were no more once-upon-a-time beginnings. The queerness of existing close to a man, the heady exhilaration of being mistress in a house of her own, had faded off into a long stretch of negative living. Now nothing was clear cut and definable; Cissie felt as if she wandered in a fog. She was that matron she'd longed to be, but she was still spinster-plain and he never did intercourse and she would never have a child or taste the thrill of outwitting Death. She supposed you could call it an original life, but she wasn't strong enough or confident enough to enjoy it. What shall I do? she asked herself. It would have been a thousand times better to have stayed single, to have remained herself, part of a pattern she understood. You might be unhappy, lonely, but there was no secret shame in spinsterhood. Others had managed the part honourably. Everyone else seemed to be someone — why wasn't she? Even Harry, who had cheated her of a proper life, didn't suffer as she did. Harry was a husband who didn't touch his wife; Cissie was merely a wife, untouched. Unrelated to anyone but herself.

In the struggle to pierce the fog of nothingness that threatened to wipe her out, Cissie's face screwed tighter, her voice grew harsher. Now *they* had reappeared, compounded; she'd been mistaken to think she could escape their judgment by moving from Wellington. In Auckland there was always an eye that scorned her, a mouth that mocked her failure. Now *them* could mean anyone at all: those wretched Maoris in the gutter; the orphaned older Tempe; Rachel Hunt, the Jewess, to whom Cissie represented Society; the legendary Blanche Dean, to whom Harry wrote without fail every week.

Cissie was only at peace when she tended her garden. Pacing its formal walks, snipping unruly stems to order and pulling up weeds she felt at ease. In the garden she was secure. Its familiar flowers were her friends; she lavished them with all her thwarted mother-love. The fuchsias she whimsically termed lady's ear drops were fed a lush diet of cow-pats and night-soil and pigeon droppings laced with rotten leaves. Her double yellow Provence rose had bloomed extravagantly after she buried a dead fox at its roots.

But Cissie's rockery comforted her most. Cruel plants grew there. The aloe was her special pet. Regularly she knelt before it, weeding with relish, pulling up the grass that grew about it studiously, yet somehow carelessly, for she always managed to tear her skin or prick her fingers on its thorny leaves. Their edges were as sharp as the bread knife. She winced as she stabbed the soft inner flesh under a nail. Yet she smiled, too, for the pain was curiously pleasant; she loved the big ugly plant.

But even the garden was flawed and, for this, Cissie had only herself to blame. For a reason she didn't understand, a selection of native plants and trees must grow there, too. In Cissie's garden was the kowhai with its spring-time cascades of golden bells and the wineberry-tree whose bunched fruit resembled small grapes.

Because of these usurpers that she herself had introduced, when she walked in the garden, particularly at evening, Cissie sometimes felt Linda to be near; felt it was Linda's garden as much as her own. At evening everything was different. The pine-trees and the darker forest behind them seemed to push close. There were strange sounds and smells — not the hot day-time scent of pinks and roses now, but something too fresh and raw. Though it was imagination, of course. Linda was dead. That glimpse of paleness you'd been frightened to look at straight, wasn't her dress but the fronds of the silver tree-fern you were proud of. And day-time or evening, the kowhai was a pretty tree; like a laburnum, and from its branches you hung coconut husks filled with sugar and water for the birds. And Cissie's wineberry jelly was delicious . . .

But it was after eating wineberry jelly that she took sick. That night it had tasted nicer than ever . . . Harry was happy, for his horses had won again, and Cissie thought: Perhaps he will love me tonight; perhaps there will still be a child. That night she had the attack. There was pain and a burning heat; her throat felt dry; then cramps and purging and vomiting. They put her to bed and it seemed to be always Linda's face or Tempe's bending over her. Doctor was in the room, too; Harry, as well, but afterwards Cissie only recalled Tempe and Linda.

Though she longed to die, she didn't. After they had tried everything and Doctor had given up hope and Harry had summoned Blanche Dean, mysteriously, Cissie recovered. Death let her down as much as everything else.

Soon Cissie was walking about again, and the period of sickness seemed like a dream. Though Blanche Dean and the little girls were there, things went on just the same. She still hated Tempe; still loved Harry and yearned for Death to try her again. Cissie was willing to suffer long and beautifully, if only she might be allowed choice of ailment. Excessive bleeding, child-bed fever — something like that would be perfect.

❦

Peach Groves, Peach Groves... Blanche Dean thanked God that tomorrow they'd set off. Te Aroha and its environs meant a different New Zealand, Mr Maufe assured. Thank God again, for the visit so far had been a disaster. Though when Harry had greeted her at the wharf she was sure the stay would be perfect. She was surer still when Cissie was revealed as being providentially recovered. Harry's letter had been merely an excuse to bring her to him. She had always known they were meant to be together.

When Blanche had been Betsy, and Liverpool was home, Granma sometimes whispered curious facts. Who'd have believed that two sweetmeats stuck together with sweat gave you power over any man you desired?

Sleeping three at the top and two at the bottom, under a threadbare counterpane, Bets dreamed of wedding sheets satin-stitched with love's emblems.

Life was so ugly, the prospect of the embroidery factory (where the wedding sheets were always for others) so grim, that only the fantastic certitudes of a penny sewn into a seam of the bride's gown for luck and no baby's breath in the wedding posy, no baby — even told in Gran's cracked voice — could make it bearable. Then Harry and she caught the excursion train, and what they did in the meadow — that was love, too. But love of such a splendid order that Bets never expected it to happen again.

Granma continued telling stories, and each night Betsy dreamed, and didn't wake to such a meaningless day. It was comforting to know that all the dreary everyday things — this boot, that spoon — could be seen in another light: possessed of magic, grown large, with power over the merely mortal. For "A bride lives the same number of years as there are buttons on her dress," Gran's voice avowed. A lump of sugar in your glove guaranteed sweetness all your married life . . . If things like that were true, then anything could happen. Harry and Bets might even escape the little lives they were expected to live.

And she got away — he did, too — but, somehow, her life was just as small.

A wedding turned Betsy into Blanche-proper. Though there wasn't baby's breath to cloud her bouquet of madonna lilies, soon Maud was born, then Ida.

When Harry came to visit, he pulled her down on the sofa and she kicked off her shoes and couldn't stop laughing. Dear bro' was back, and marvellously changed for the better. Everything seemed but a joke: those ridiculous potichimanie vases, the pheasant wing fire-screen with its chenille tassels. Life could be fun; having money was fun with Harry's sun-tanned hand cupping your elbow. Even George's ponderous respectability couldn't dash Blanche's mood. Though race day had to stay a secret. What happened after, as well.

And though he left her, though for years she merely had his letters, there was the sure knowledge that eventually she'd be with him again.

But she had come to New Zealand and he didn't want her. Though he'd pretended at first and greeted her fondly at the harbour, and accepted the carved emu egg with a smile.

One morning they walked in the garden. His voice was cold as he told her that what they'd done in the past was a sin. Never again, he said.

Blanche had so much love to give. Her body seemed strung together by love. She was only a puppet, moving where it led her. She had never felt so miserable, yet for the sake of love she dressed her body with care. Harry hated her and she wished she could die, yet she had never looked so comely. Sometimes, she used some of the love up on the little girls. Ida flinched from her too tight embrace, but Maud was overjoyed. Dear Maud. She was so much her mama's image that Blanche felt it to be like hugging herself.

Then, too, there was George to spend love on. For George, at a distance, was a vague figure, shadowy. He had dwindled to a miniature man, sepia-tinted, screwing his eyes at the sun, enclosed by the limits of a *repoussé* frame. He sat on the rustic seat that, larger, graced the garden at Glenelg and, if Blanche looked closely, behind him was the big bush of diosma turned dwarf as everything else. In the photo George smoked his pipe and, to Blanche at Epsom, it seemed an endearing habit . . . she could almost smell his favourite Diamond tobacco — strange how it seemed an attractive smell now, when usually she couldn't bear it.

But George wasn't enough. Though Blanche's thoughts started off dutifully wifely, she always ended up thinking of Harry. And then love stopped being sentimental. It turned cruel, and a pain sharp as an icicle dug at her heart. Love hurt too much, Blanche wasn't woman enough to bear it. She must shut Harry out; think of something safe, the more mundane the better. Of how bad the Epsom drawing-room was for singing; how the piano, though a grand, had four dumb notes.

Really, it was easy to think Harry away. Often George returned to take his place, and Blanche felt so unaccountably guilty that she must scribble at another letter. The day before they left for The Peach Groves was no exception:

". . . and thank you, dearest, for the money-order. I did not expect another so soon, but it was welcome as we go to the Maufes' tomorrow. Mr Maufe asked Maud to bring her violin with her, so I bought her a violin case as it will be rough travelling — by rail, coach and steamer. It cost eleven shillings, but now I feel easy about it. That violin was a white elephant to me all the way to New Zealand . . ."

PART THREE

The Peach Groves

1

God was good. Up here it was like being in Eden. And even more so today, when they'd set out early and started down-river in the Maufes' big barge with a cover to keep the sun off, and the little steamer tugging them along. Gliding in a floating dream: Blanche reclining on soft cushions, lazily aware of the waterfall of lace at her throat, and the fact that her bonnet was a perfect *bijou*.

The day was bright, with a cool fresh breeze. The climate here was different to Auckland's. Blanche felt so well; it was so bracing and cool. The river quivered, silver in the sun; trees hung over the water, making a thick green shade; really, she was half asleep.

Decidedly, there was a pattern. How glad she was that they had come. The Peach Groves was a most lovely place. Within a mile and a quarter east were high mountains whose colour changed every few minutes, presenting a different range of light and shadow, but always most beautiful. Close to the house, winding round it, was the Thames River or, rather, a branch of it called the Waihou, which Mr Maufe said meant "new water".

All was for the best. Blanche felt better; thought of Harry didn't hurt as much. Mr Maufe was an ideal host, sparing himself no effort for their comfort and entertainment. They'd had a glorious picnic already, up in the mountains. Now they had come down-river to the place that had inspired Mr Maufe to call his property The Peach Groves. Here, in the wars of the sixties, a Maori village had been ravaged. All that remained of that former occupation were groves of neglected peach-trees. Laden branches sagged earthward; the grass was clotted with fallen fruit abandoned to the wild pigs.

They spread their tablecloth in a picturesque spot. As well as peach-trees there were weeping willows that hung over the steamer and barge. Champagne tasted nicer than ever out-of-doors; the pigeon pies were delicious. Blanche knew that her letters would never give George the least idea of the luxuriant foliage. There were no snakes and no wild flowers, either, though some of the native trees and bushes flowered splendidly.

After the fruit tarts and jellies they boiled up a kettle of tea over a fire of bark and leaves. Then Mr Maufe enjoyed his pipe and Master Octavius Maufe fell asleep and the little girls played tag between the trees, while the ladies gathered up the soiled crocks. Old Mrs Maufe was a true artist, hopelessly un-domesticated. Her daughters appeared fond enough of her, though. They humoured her eccentricities and called her "Little Mother".

Each tree was encircled with a wave of peachy

perfume. The wind blew, and the trees seemed to breathe in great scented gusts. As the afternoon wore on, the smell became heavier, cloying . . . soon they had all emulated Octavius, and were fast in the arms of Somnus. All, that is, except Blanche who didn't feel sleepy at all. It was horrid to lie there so still, but she had to. Outwardly, in the open where it showed, you must be the same as everyone else.

So Blanche lay under the peach-trees and pretended sleep, and didn't see the small creatures that moved among the grass — ant and grub and hairy-kneed spider. Beetles pierced the earth with passages; the humble-bee burrowed, too, to build its thimble-like cells; whirligigs and lacewings flitted in mazy dance on the surface of the river, but Blanche paid them no heed. The intrigues of their miniature world didn't concern her — till a mosquito bit her neck and she stopped feigning sleep.

And then she wished she hadn't. For her eyes flew open and, at first (despite the mosquito), she still felt at peace. It was a pleasure party, perfectly blissful. Everyone wearing best clothes, everything nasty far away. The others slept on — Mrs Maufe, snoring under her veil; Miss Ethel nuzzling Miss Queenie's aesthetic shoulder; Octavius curled hedgehog-tight . . . Ida and her ridiculous doll, dear Tempe, dear Maud . . .

Then Blanche's fond gaze focused on Mr Maufe, and suddenly everything was ruined. For he was awake, too, though he didn't know she knew. He was looking at the little girls. No, he was looking at Maud. He was smiling, yet not — his lip was curled back, almost you might say in a snarl. It gave

Blanche goose-pimples. It was a secret look, one you took care not to wear in public.

And all the time Maud slept on like an angel, and the water lapped rhythmically at the bank — sometimes khaki-coloured, sometimes silver, and the darting insects flashed above it. The sun filtered through the willows to dapple the sleepers' skin: they were marked with jelly-fish blobs and tiger-stripes of sunshine. And all the hairs on Mr Maufe's head, and his moustache, and the little hairs on his wrists glinted like silk. Perhaps it was the fault of the hairs as much as his expression, but, whatever it was, Blanche couldn't help it: she looked at him and he was looking at Maud, and he wasn't a dear old man, well-connected, someone worthwhile to know. Instead, he was a wild animal.

But, of course, it was a trick of the light. A lady should be wary of the sun. Nothing was worse than a tan. Blanche shut her eyes quickly, but the dancing motes still teased her — they were there under her eyelids, but only for a bit. Soon she felt quite calm. It was a mistake, definitely. The Earl of Annersley's nephew had stayed at The Peach Groves to learn farming. When the maids laid the table they didn't touch the silver with their fingers, but used a shammy so you never saw a thumb-mark. There were that many books. In any case, Mr Maufe doted on Maud . . .

When they woke they gathered baskets of peaches. It was a pleasant pastime, reaching up into the swags of pointed leaves that smelled vaguely of marzipan, to pluck the creamy-greenish, rose-flushed fruit. Some peaches were glazed with gum, a few were laced with cobwebs; ants studded those that lay in the grass. Blanche held out a peach to the sun, and it was covered with silvery down. She rubbed the peach against her cheek and there was a velvety itch, a prickle. And the lovely smell. You couldn't help but be tempted to eat. You tore the skin off with jabs of your thumbnail. You bit, and juice ran down your crooked arm and into your sleeve. Half eaten, its pitted stone revealed, a peach resembled a strange flower. You were sticky-fingered after eating; you had peach flesh in your fingernails.

They picked a lot, for Miss Queenie Maufe said peaches were excellent preserved in brandy. Then they started up-river, stopping under some trees that hung over the water to have their tea.

They had come down the river like lightning, but it took a long time going up. They passed Te Aroha about nine; they did not get home till one o'clock in the morning.

Didn't Blanche wish George had been there. They were such a jolly party and the river was so beautiful that, looking back, it seemed like a dream — their gliding along it all day.

🌿

It was The Peach Groves, but — like Uncle Harry and Mount Eden — it was different to what Ida expected. For a while, though, things seemed exactly right. That last little bit of journeying to Mr Maufe's other New Zealand couldn't have been bettered. After the train and the coach and the steamer, the waggonette was waiting. "Not long now," said Mr Maufe as the horses started off, and his voice cut off Ida's dreaming. They'd travelled all day and now it was night, but pressed close to Mama she jerked awake. Her eyes ached and her body felt wobbly, but her mind was fresh and alive. She concentrated on the strangeness. All the scents were different, all the shapes were new; Ida didn't know where she was.

But as the waggonette lumbered along it was perfect — the approach to some Gothic domain. Night had swooped on petty detail, and they might have been anywhere; even entered the fairy-tale at last. The waggonette's lanterns fanned out in fitful ghost-gleams; they travelled through black velvet shades. All about them seemed to be the tale's regulation forest, and from it now and then a ruffled branch extended, and something daintily tendrilled — portion of which vine, what creeper? Of course, there must be moss and ferns and small streamlets trickling, for they travelled through a damp dark world that, even by day, wouldn't admit much light. Who were they, where did the waggonette lead them? Ida shivered happily, as they moved down that sinister lane, the name of which surely featured on no map.

Then they rounded a bend and the house jumped forward. At a time when even candlelight would have been too bright, there seemed to be a lamp at every window.

All about you was the flurry of a new arrival, and you played up to it — staggered a bit, rubbed your eyes. "Poor little love," crooned Miss Ethel as she pinned you against her and you never wanted to be a lady — a pale person, Miss Ethel, like those scurrying things you surprised under rocks in the garden. Miss Queenie was sharper, you didn't like her, though you admired her petersham belt. Her kiss was dry, just a peck. You didn't have to wipe it off, like Miss Ethel's, but somehow you felt insulted.

There was hot milk and cinnamon toast, and things improved. The strange lady's eye-shade looked promising, as did young Mr Maufe's swollen thumb.

Then Ida must have fallen asleep, for suddenly everything was different. Servant hands were holding her; she was being carried up a flight of stairs. This time the bed was a big one that held Maud as well. The sheets had a pleasant smell, something like lilac. Queechy shared her pillow.

By day there wasn't much mystery: it was mainly the fault of the house. The Peach Groves wasn't a pretty residence, by any means. It wasn't elegant, like Uncle's house; though, like Uncle's, it was made of wood. Mr Maufe's house, however, sought to disguise the fact; its woodenness being artfully persuaded to resemble quite something else.

The first thing you noticed were all the little bricks — trembly white lines arranged so neatly on an ox-blood red ground. And there was a lot of fret-work trim like the braid on Ida's merino dress, and barley-sugar columns like the ones on the merry-go-round, and other columns like they had in ancient Greece.

But the verandah floor was tessellated elegantly in a pattern of stars, and the front door came all the way from England. That door was a beauty — the maid must clean the brass every day. And there was a marble door-step that you weren't allowed to scrub, but had to wash with a solution of starch.

Even where the door-step curved under — you must wash the dirt out of there as well.

The maid was nice. Nicer to talk to than almost anyone. Cook was all right, too. She gave Ida a bun just out of the oven, and let her stir the Spotted Dick.

And there was Oc — nice as well, who wasn't a man but a boy, despite sometimes needing to shave. Now that Ida knew him, his head didn't seem so out-size; known, he was calmer and didn't so regularly flex his thumb. He was their friend — Maud liked him, too. He told them of King Grisly-beard and Deerfoot; he showed them the large leaf called the bushman's friend. Oc and Maud and Ida, though, had a better use for these leaves than lavatory paper for — doubled over, leaf-tip pierced by stem — they did for fairy boats. The stream they sailed on was at the bottom of the garden. The bush started there, and Oc showed them the tree-fern that was a silvery colour under its fronds, and Oc knew that Deerfoot had used those fronds to mark the track when he travelled at night. Hanging from the trees were thick strands of supplejack, and it was thrilling to take a grip of the lower end of a vine and give it a tug to see it held firm and run back with it and then take off. Deerfoot's vine had carried him safely across the rapids so he might escape the enemy Shawanoes.

But when Ida met Oc inside the house, or when the grown-ups were about, he was another. Not Oc at all, but merely Octavius — Mr Maufe the younger, who bound books. Unlike Oc, Octavius had a head that was certainly swollen and you felt you would scream if he didn't leave his thumb alone. Poor Octavius. He hardly spoke above a whisper, and he wasn't a boy like Oc, but a man who was unfortunate.

Inside the house, too, were Queenie and Ethel. One's kiss was wet, the other's dry. One wore woolly undies, even on hot days, and retired to a room scented with zinc cream. The other's room had holy pictures and a jar of peacock feathers.

Ida enjoyed peeping, but she got a fright when she looked in the box-room. For someone was there, and it was the lady with the eye-shade. Wifey, Little Mother, Mrs Maufe.

But those names didn't suit her. Her real name was Zillah, which did. By then — when they'd been properly introduced — Ida had stopped being frightened and her eyes moved about the room. It was a box-room full of trunks and portmanteaux, but it was something else as well. The room was dark, but Zillah sat at a table before a sketch-block and her hand held a pen. Regularly, its nib dipped into an ink-well and, without prompting, strange pictures appeared. They weren't ordinary drawings, though. Not the Jonathan apple rendered faithfully, or the ox-eye daisy got to the life. Ida edged closer; Zillah seemed to have forgotten she was there.

And on the page a little girl wandered. All about her was a thicket of lines. Her skin was so white and the harsh lines, so black, made brambles and thorn-trees that would tear her whiteness to shreds. Zillah's pen moved faster, and now the little girl's hair was tangled with the thorns and you wondered if she'd ever get free. And then another shape started coming through the brambles towards her; not a comforting shape: the little girl drew back.

Then the pen seemed to be scratching in someone else; someone whose hands might come to the child's aid. Ida hoped so, and it seemed so, for they looked kind hands, helpful . . . now there were cuffs and a sleeve; now shoulders and the start of a chin. But that was all — no more, for Zillah's pen spluttered to a stop. A trail of ink-blots fell on the child and what happened to her? — did she escape her pursuer or not? Zillah didn't seem concerned either way. She shut the drawing-book briskly, and pushed it aside. She sighed, as if she'd been wandering a long time in a forest, herself. She bade Ida come closer, for she couldn't see her clearly. It was her weak eyes, Zillah said. She must take care.

Even when you knew her, Zillah could frighten you. There was something about her that baffled description. Without warning her eyes would stop seeing you, and her face screw up as if something hurt. "Take care," she would say. "You must take care." Trees were especially enemies. They waited to pounce on your life-stream to suck you dry. Once there was a pepper-tree and Zillah sat under it and contracted rheumatics.

But Zillah wasn't consistent. Like Oc, who eluded you as Octavius, she could turn into a stranger. Often she was but Mrs Maufe, a silly old lady, bumbling, who disregarded Zillah's warnings and sat under the willows at the picnic. Sometimes the pictures she drew were merely scary in a regular way. Death rocked the cradle of doomed infants; no one worse than Gentle Jesus waited to pounce.

Then, too, there was Mr Maufe. His sort of frightening was different. This time there seemed no reason for fear. He was still the kindly gentleman

116

he'd been at Epsom: the little girls' friend, Master Bob's in particular.

But his eyes behind the pebble-glass were hard; they didn't match his wheedling voice. Evil was sickening when it stayed a half thing — soft and musty, clumsily-clinging.

Tempe was at The Peach Groves, too: she frightened Ida, as well. And perhaps Tempe's style of frightening was worst of all. For her eyes didn't chill you; she uttered no warning nor drew the threatened child again and again. Instead, she was so demure, so perfectly the neatly buttoned young lady who was Mama's confidant.

Yet, despite Tempe's looks and ability to play at willing listener, how could Mama like her? She had floated in the pool with only an excuse for clothes on; she let Uncle kiss her. She'd kicked Queechy aside when the doll lay, forgotten, on the path (it was this that turned Ida against her). Tempe was deceitful, sly, unchaste. She told lies.

She made the White and Pink Terraces, nominated eighth wonder of the world, sound like lumps of coconut ice. She was always on about heroes who were Maoris, when there weren't any about at all. She said that at Te Aroha, where you went for the baths, all the people — men, women, children — went into the water together, and there were introductions over floating tables. Decidedly, Tempe was a liar. There would be a fancy ball, it was true, but where would all the people she described in such detail come from? Would the ladies really loop up their petticoats and trudge for miles in galoshes; would the gentleman like a prince in black velvet attend, and all those other lesser gentlemen who were even now practising waltz steps in drawing-rooms hidden away up-river? Perhaps it was true, probably not. Though there might be all those gents in patent leather pumps close at hand. For there *was* Te Aroha and, even nearer, there was the little town that owned the church where Queenie and Ethel snapped lily stalks for God. It was here, Tempe reckoned there'd be a circus. A real one, with elephant and dog-faced boy. Ida had never been to the circus, but Maud had. Once Mama and Papa took her to one in Adelaide, and she saw the Moss-haired Girl and Monty, Untameable Abyssinian Lion.

2

Who am I, what am I? Oc pondered, and wished there was someone to answer. The mirror didn't help. It only showed the large head and the little body, the stains on his waistcoat, his nibbled nails. Fingernail biting was one of his habits. He'd always had habits, they seemed like old friends. A particular favourite was combing his hair. He'd sit at the polished table, if the drawing-room happened to be empty, and put his head down and comb and comb. The scurf fell like snow; the storm raged all over the table, but his face stayed quite safe.

But: *Melon* said the boys at school, and now his face was on fire. Now it was a hunted thing, the lip quivering, the eyes stinging. *Dummy, Blockhead,* said the boys and he'd thought school would mean something else. Thought: I will cross my ankles and with elbows tucked in learn to be a scholar. But Mama sent him into a savage land. They were hounds tearing at the soft grey hare. "Oh please," he cried, but they had no mercy — their boots kept stabbing his side. And that day behind the cricket pitch after he'd missed the sure catch . . . they had hawthorn branches and their hands kept flailing, falling from the bright blue sky. Their laughter was beautiful, they were heroes, but the thorns cut his skin. "Oh please," Oc cried again, but the prefects flogged on. His back felt sticky, hawthorn petals were pretty in spring. *Little beast*, they sneered. *Blockhead.* But he loved them, the great boys in flannel trousers. They were gods with their thorn sticks — strong-limbed, small-headed with noses like Greek heroes. His undervest absorbed most of the blood, though his shirt was stained faintly in places.

Oc learned. He was the insect that blended with the leaf, the ptarmigan that merged with the hillside. He became a sort of mascot; they said their *Melons* differently — sometimes it was even *Old Oc* : a character, skin like a rhino. But: Why? he sobbed, his teeth biting into the sheet as the cool darkness washed away dormitory, beds, other boys. Home, I want to be home, he sobbed silently. And he remembered, without meaning to, how at home, once, they'd read a poem. It was a petition from the sugar-making slaves, humbly addressed to the consumers of sugar. Mama and Oc always started crying at the very first verse:

> *You no wish that we should suffer,*
> *Gentle Massa, we are sure:*
> *You quite willing we be happy,*
> *If you see it in your power.*

Dear Mama. He loved her, she was so ugly. Her mouth was soft, like a blundering moth. She was always kissing him. "Tinker-tailor," she said to his buttons; "This little Piggy," she said to his toes. He would sit on her lap before the fire. There were faces in the flames — Napoleon, King Herod — and sometimes a hiss, sometimes fire-cracker sparks. Their cheeks rubbed together and he had the frog in his throat, so she took off her stocking and wound it round his throat like a muffler. He wore it to bed to keep out froggy; her smell stayed close to him all night.

But there were enemies at home, even when he was King. Queenie and Ethel. Papa.

"You are a dreamer, Octavius," said Papa. The pater did not dream, he had never seen angels; he went gladly to school. Papa was the young heir, one of the flannelled heroes. He excelled at cricket and hare-and-hounds; he skated on the pond, he was popular, a sure thing at everything scholastic. He never left his fat at dinner, the *Book of Martyrs* could not scare him. But there was something about Papa that put Oc off. He was fishy, your hand slithered from him. Oc hated the way he spoke of Mama. "Wifey," he said, "converses with spirits." The words were all right — it was his tone. He meant Mama was cracked, that she'd be sent to Bethlem Hospital. Incurables were there; but Mama wasn't an indigent lunatic. "No, no, Papa," cried Oc. "Say you don't mean it." Though you knew it wasn't true, Papa must say the "Not true" for you. But he wouldn't, he kept smiling. And you knew he hated you, that he was another great boy of the Fifth; yet at the same time he was a very small boy — somehow he was the smallest fag getting his own back (but for what?) as he started you off on a crying fit.

Even if she didn't see you any more she was still

Old Ugly who'd kissed you kindly and rubbed Russian tallow on your chest. Now and then the spirits let her go. Mama came back and you ate toast together and worried over Little Nell. But then she'd be off again (now it was inspirational writing, next came sewing on canvas): Papa smiled again. Oh not Bethlem. Margaret Nicholson, who'd attempted to stab his late Majesty, was there; likewise Hadfield, who'd shot at the King in Drury Lane Theatre. But Papa smiled broader and bared his animal teeth. "It is an admirable place, dear Octavius," he said nicely. You could take tea with the keepers at a small weekly charge. Good table-beer was allowed. In the hall of the Hospital for your edification were Caius Gabriel Cibber's celebrated figures of raving and melancholy madness. "It might be for the best if we packed the old girl off," said Papa. He was joking, of course. Queenie and Ethel giggled nervously. I will kill him, thought Oc, but he had learned; the heroes had taught him well. He blended like the insect, the bird; Papa never knew how he felt. Not then; not now, in the new land across the sea.

"But what will become of the boy?" asked Papa. For Octavius was not practical. He'd brought home the medal for good conduct, but in the business of living he was pure dunce. There was cash enough, however, Papa supposed — smiling again (oh, how Papa loved to show off his teeth) — for the family to support a gentleman of leisure. But even a young blood must spend his days somehow. You couldn't merely look out of the window and consider the different colour of grass on the opposite side of the world, though it seemed sensible enough to Oc to do just that.

He had to have an interest, said Papa. When he began binding the world came alive again.

Books were as much Oc's friends as the habits. They stood snugly arranged on their shelf, the small swag of dust that fell regularly before them carefully swept away. Their spines were sprigged with gold curlicles and literary lettering. Little Nell was there, and Deerfoot, too. Some books were there, though, not because of the people or the facts inside them. Some he kept for sentiment; some books that you never bothered to read — *A Manual of Bee-keeping, Heroes of Hebrew History* — were poems in themselves. From the leaves of books like that, fell pansies and roses and maidenhair fern; love-tokens pressed by time to the same drab sepia, the same tissue-paper fragility. Oc couldn't bear to throw them away. A page in *The Popular Educator* was marked by a butterfly's wing.

But he hadn't looked at his books for a long time. Papa had brought most of them from Auckland and Papa made books something you flinched from. "How about this one, Octavius?" he'd ask. "Do you reckon you can save it?" Oc's nimble fingers did miracles and the tattered pages turned fresh. But Oc's eyes mustn't read a word, for it was filthy, he did not understand. But the mad dizzy feeling kept coming and he couldn't help it — he bore no responsibility: his eyes wouldn't stop reading.

Away from the house he felt all right. He lay in the grass at the bottom of the garden, he shut his eyes and the feverish feeling abated. Oc stopped hating them — Papa and himself and the girl who was only a body spread-eagled, morocco-bound. The charnel house stench was absorbed by the sky and Oc was a child at Mama's knee. He said "Gentle Jesus" and the other old prayers, and Grisly-beard and the Princess came back.

Then suddenly the Princess left the page, she stepped from Oc's mind. Visitors were coming and the maids chased the dust and Zillah was buttoned away and Wifey, Little Mother took her place. He ran to hide but Papa caught him half-way up the stairs and called "Come down you rascal, Octavius. Where are your manners?"

Mrs Dean's blouse was marvellously shot-silk and changed its colour each time she moved. As well, there was a young lady, Miss Wimperis, whom Oc did not like. But the little roly-poly girl's gaze was tolerable, even though she focused on his head. Then Queenie stepped aside and he saw her. Papa's hand was on her shoulder; she was lovely.

The fairy-tale was true. She was Snow-drop, risen from the coffin of glass, though they introduced her as Maud.

He would do anything for her. It was foul that Papa should touch her. He was Oc Maufe with a clumsy body, but she made him feel strong. When he was with her he felt confident. But he had to be stronger, he'd need the fabled strength of Hercules to get free, for inside the house he was bewitched; once past the front door Papa spelled him and he was reduced to Octavius, problem son.

Maud, who was lovely as a princess, did not laugh at him. She listened with interest when he told her how perfect Home would eventually be. She had given him hope. Soon he'd be strong enough to say

No to Papa; he'd rip the books apart and tear the words to tiny pieces, so that the filth floated away, dandruff-small. And Papa would turn into his subject, Queenie and Ethel would curtsy low, for Oc was King again and the siren voices had stopped lisping — she'd come downstairs from the box-room marvellously restored, she'd be Mama again, and they'd live happily ever after and rule The Peach Groves together.

✿

Certainly, Tempe was a liar but the circus was true. The night before the evening when Mr Maufe would take them, excitement stopped Ida from sleeping. Till a string of ballet girls drifted under her eyelids and then she started to dream. At first the dream was powder-puff pretty, as delicate as a butterfly's wing. The ballet girls kicked their legs and their net skirts were full of sequins, they had rag roses in their hair. Then they unhooked little fingers to flutter separately — the pale one like a pearly moth, the cheeky one with a beauty-spot, whose skirt fluffed out dandelion-clockwise . . . But the clowns, painted and nose-pasted, were better still. Oh, they were funny, doing comic wrestling and the nightingale twitters. Ida and Queechy applauded, and next thing they straddled the padded back of the roundabout cockerel, which was when things started going wrong. For the cockerel turned its head and its beak was cruel, its eye glinted coldly. But Queechy said the magic name. "New Zealand," she said, though it sounded like "Museum", and because she said it the roundabout

125

stopped whirling and Ida and Queechy were free. The nice things were there again, exotic yet cosy, like the brass plate from Benares on the mantel. All the danger was reserved for someone other than yourself: Chinky-Chinaman performing pigtail acrobatics on the slanting high-wire; Captain Schneider, whose gold teeth were studded with diamonds, who shaved himself in the lions' cage. Everything was silver-paper bright again; the screams from the switchback were muted. Ida and Queechy shared jelly babies and wondered at the Irish Giant. The Bearded Lady threw them a kiss and they came to the very last booth. In there was the best thing of all (perhaps Latiefa, Queen of Reptiles) and you must hurry, for the roundabout music had started again — the four-abreast gallopers might get you. Inside, though, the booth wasn't peppermint-stick striped; inside it was only dark . . .

By the time Ida and Maud were spooning up porridge, the dream had faded to a memory of Captain Schneider's dazzling incisors. Though the excitement remained. All through the day it was there, and anticipation proved so pleasurable that it was almost a disappointment when evening fell, and they climbed into the waggonette and set off.

This time their party was a small one, for Octavius disliked circuses, while the Misses Maufe felt themselves above them, and Wifey had retired to the box-room to draw.

It didn't take long to reach the little town, and as they drew up at the Recreation Ground, Mr Maufe seemed suddenly important. So many gentlemen raised their hats; so many ladies nodded in greeting.

Ida was proud to be seen sharing his carriage with its dimpled leather seats and straight-backed coach-man. It was so much smarter than the commonplace buggies and drags that lesser mortals rode in. Ida felt smug as she recalled that at The Peach Groves, though rarely used, were several other varieties of elegant vehicle. The brougham did for wet weather; the phaeton swept genteelly down in the middle, so that a lady might enter or alight without fear of exposing her ankles.

Attached to the big iron gate was a poster cram-med with curly black letters. GREATEST SHOW ON EARTH it said. CIRCUS, MENAGERIE, FREAK-SHOW AND WILD AUSTRALIA. As well as the words there were pictures. The lady with the Jap umbrella skipped on the flying trapeze. The elephant trumpetted cockily; Leo narrowed his eyes. Ida would have liked to look longer, but the others swept her away. Now they were walking up a path towards lights and the vague shapes of tents. Everyone hurried forward, all in best clothes, and there were so many interesting smells — the ladies' floral scents and powders, cigar smoke and some-thing like moth-balls, mixed with the night smells of the trees and grass, and an itchy feeling of excite-ment — that you knew it to be a special occasion. Nearer and nearer came the lights, and Ida felt the same as she did when they walked with Nurse at Glenelg, and the sea at the end of the street kept getting bluer and sloppier, till she couldn't bear it, but shrugged off Nursie's hand and ran to meet it. The lights had the same effect now. Beside her, Maud gave a shiver, and then it was lovely to have a sister, for each seemed to know the other's feelings.

Without warning, they held hands and ran helter-skelter before the sedate grown-ups.

But there wasn't a switchback or a razzle-dazzle; not even a set of hurdy-gurdy gallopers. There were, however, carbide-gas flares and a stall selling toffee apples. They queued at the ticket office and first was the Menagerie which was a let-down, for there wasn't a lion or an elephant, only monkeys and a stuffed Tasmanian tiger. Though the camel made up for it a bit. He had a tassel and a row of pompoms round his saddle and the camel-boy was brown as a berry in leopard-skin drawers. The Freaks were good, too. It wasn't an Irish giant, but Chang-the-Chinese, who was also the Tattooed Man. And fancy being the little girl born covered in spots. Though taking a turn as Bearded Lady might be worse.

Then they were sitting in their seats and Mr Maufe seemed improved, for the chocolates he'd chosen were expensive. Even Tempe wasn't too bad. She had spunk, certainly, for the camel-boy had given her a wink — Ida had seen, and Tempe had the cheek to wink back. Ida sighed happily, and passed the choc box along to Mama, and there were a series of paradiddles from the kettledrum and the lady-pianist did vamping like mad. White light poured down on the ring and the man dressed for dinner cracked his whip, and everything happened as it should. The Equestrian Nymph graced the galloping horse's back on one quivering leg; Miss M'hamedin writhed out her Beautiful Serpentine Dance, and there were acrobats in shocking pink tights. But the lady with the Jap umbrella didn't turn up, and WILD AUSTRALIA was just this man in a singlet chopping a log, and Tempe ruined the Dancing Ducks when she reckoned they only skipped because they stood on a hot plate while someone lit a fire underneath.

Yet, flawed as it was, the circus had power while they watched it to weld them into a try at happy family. Chocolate dissolving on your tongue, Mr Maufe and Tempe were people you were fond of; it didn't matter that Maud was Mama's pet not you. But out in the cold again, though her hands still tingled from clapping the Grand Parade, Ida felt suddenly lonely. Over her head the grown-ups mocked the magic with casual phrases. The acrobats were deemed excellent, Miss M'hamedin, too; but though the Nymph was a trier (especially in the Spanish trot), last year's Blondin on Horseback out-classed her. It was a pity he died when his steed fell on him at morning rehearsal.

Now, with every step Ida took, she distanced herself further from the close-knit tinsel world. The grown-ups kept chattering and beside her Maud was humming, but shadows pressed near. Soon the carbide flares were reduced to pin-pricks, then snuffed out entirely by a turn of the path. Peach Groves bound, the ladies' perfume didn't smell so pungent; there was an awful feeling of melancholy. You held Mama's hand, but knew yourself to be irredeemably separate. Ida felt as bad as she had when the *Valetta* drew away from the wharf and Papa turned more and more into that doll, mechanically waving.

And for an instant she almost ran back. She was sure everything stayed the same, waiting for her return. Chang-the-Chinese perpetually slipped off his satin dressing-gown to reveal the reproduction of the Last Supper on his back and the representation of the Crucifixion on his chest; the Spotted Girl mournfully extended her polka-dot palms for inspection; the Bearded Lady sat queen-like in her booth, unaware of the biscuit crumbs in her elf-locks.

But, swaying homeward in the waggonette, Ida was unexpectedly comforted. She was plagued again by memory of a pair of classy jewelled teeth. They snapped at her companionably all the way home: she didn't feel so lonely. Only when she was curled up in bed were the gold and diamond dentures framed by lips and the spiralled tips of a waxed moustache; only then did the rest of dashing Captain Schneider appear, profusely braided and brass-buttoned. Ida welcomed him gladly. In last night's dream he'd lathered his chin in the lions' cage and wielded his razor languidly. The same thing happened now. The bars of the cage gleamed slippery as liquorice straps; the lions roared on cue . . .

Dreams were dependable where reality wasn't. There might be nasty bits that verged on nightmare, but by breakfast you'd usually forgotten. In any case, you could dream consciously, by day. Ida dodged Maud and Oc to sit beneath the lilac-tree and invent the best circus of all. In this one there'd be twin elephants, Rajah and Nero, as well as Captain S. and his lions; there'd be the lady with the Jap umbrella as well as the Equestrian Nymph. Soon the drums were paradiddling nicely. The Nymph didn't flinch as the first paper hoop was shattered.

All morning the drum beats pounded redly in

Ida's brain, they stabbed at her heart. She lay under the lilac-tree and the earth pounded, too, though perhaps it was only her breathing. The morning slipped away statically, busily; she felt secure enough to smile with satisfaction. In her hidey-hole, creating a circus of her own, Ida knew she had no need of anyone — not even Queechy — for company.

But the acrobats were interrupted by lunch. And after tapioca pudding Tempe whispered in Mama's ear. Mama said, "How kind of you to offer," but Ida didn't want to go. How could walking with Tempe compare with big-top dreaming? But: "Certainly not," said Mama. All that solitary mooning was morbid.

You were an ingrate, an unnatural child. You knew what Mama would have said if you weren't visiting, if she'd been Pepper-box in the drawing-room with Papa. So many times you'd put your ear to the door, and listened coldly as if she spoke of a stranger: ". . . and all that pain, all the suffering and what for? . . . not a trace of me in her, and I don't care, you can't make me. I can't bring myself to feel a thing." Poor Mama. Poor Ida: Freckled nose, frizz-bush hair . . . I declare I despair . . . Why not like Maud?

Sulkily, Ida sucked the elastic chin-strap of her sun-hat and tagged Tempe and Maud round the roses. But it started to be an adventure when they veered off the path. Soon the forest turned strange and their eyes stopped seeing it clearly. It was the fault of the queer green light — for the forest latticed the sky, and the sun slunk in warily, watery, sometimes to swim through the greenness, though more often to sink. And, as well, there was such quantity of vegetation — layer upon layer, each manically leaved and berried and nested with variety of bird — that your eyes only coped by sliding off detail. Which meant that, seeable, the forest was merely an anonymous moss-green blur. Through it, in follow-my-leader formation, moved Tempe and Maud and Ida. Ida's hand held fast to the hem of Maud's pinafore; Ida's eyes focused there, too. That way the blur dissolved further; that way you might stay safe.

For terror waited constantly to pounce. The roundabout cockerel had cruel eyes and the Babes in the Wood had perished. Maud would look lovely crying with hunger, then lying down, then dying. Perhaps it would happen — the redbreasts managing to sing mournfully as they spread their coverlet of leaves; probably not. For Tempe moved surely, as if their path was ordained, and perhaps her confidence did the trick. At their approach particular bushes shivered invitingly, certain branches beckoned. "This way," Tempe murmured dreamily, decidedly. Obediently, the forest admitted them.

Soon it was easy going. They were descending, and through the trees Ida saw a road. Tempe smiled triumphantly and told them that it was the one they'd travelled last night — the road that led to the circus. "Surprised?" she asked tauntingly, and now Ida wasn't fond of her at all. Tempe was as captive as everyone else. She had spunk and a funny look in her eyes, but the grown-up world had got her all the same. She was bold and defied Aunt Cissie's world of convention, but, by leading Uncle to her room, she lost all the freedom she'd won. Why must Tempe always turn passive, why hold him to her by letting him crush her?

The walk towards the tents wasn't mysterious with blue sky overhead. Pines could be miserable trees; the grass at their feet was shrivelled. There were several rickety caravans, and the snot-nosed children drew back to giggle at their approach. It was stupid of Tempe to have brought them here. By day they weren't proper circus people at all.

Chang wasn't Chinese now he'd left off his eye-paint, and not nearly so tall without his boots. The Bearded Lady slumped in her booth instead of sitting queenly; and her chin was bald, without even a hint of five o'clock shadow. Miss M'hamedin squatted before the Spotted Girl, carefully apportioning the day's fresh quota of dot with indelible pencil.

But Tempe moved past the sham freaks, unconcerned. They weren't what had brought her here, it was plain to see. Who was it then? Surely not the ring-master or the Dancing Ducks' attendant. Then Ida saw him step forward to meet her. He'd left off the leopard-skin drawers, but even regulation moleskin couldn't disguise his berry-brownness. He was still the camel-boy who'd winked.

3

Linda had guided her. *This way*, Mother called, *over here*, and the roots of the trees gave up trying to trip them, the prickly creepers drew back. Trees and ferns and razor-edged grasses turned docile; there was a path again, and: *Here, Tempe*, crooned Mother (who was a whisper riding in your ear, a hand securing tricky liana). The path went on, and: *This way, this way*: obediently the forest opened up. Soon the trees let in the sky again; soon the grass stopped nipping their ankles, and at the bottom of the slope was the road. "Surprised?" she asked Ida and Maud.

She'd had to bring them, for they were her only excuse for getting away. Blanche needed Tempe beside her constantly; Blanche didn't know how she'd manage alone. Lately, though, Blanche had felt better. "It must be Peach Groves air," she confided, her cheeks a fetching shade of pink, her eyes brimming forget-me-not blue. Then all the colour drained away, and she looked as if she chewed on a lemon. "Ah, I do miss him so," she mourned with a touch of la Duse. Oh God, was she going to cry again? — but careful, you must be clever, for it wasn't time to show yourself yet. Tempe was so nice. She patted poor Blanche's hand and made cluck-cluck noises with her tongue, while: Damn and blast her eyes, said Tempe's brain. Damn Harry, too . . . but: Oh, I want him, thought Tempe, while: "How I long for dear bro'," said Blanche.

It was awful when you had to go without someone to love you. Tempe felt strange, her skin went itchy. At night in bed she scratched till her legs felt on fire and the skin was all little flakes. Her pillow was one big pebble, then it was lumpy; she tossed all night, she couldn't find a comfortable place. She wanted someone so bad — Harry, of course, though anyone would do — that her body felt stiff, as if it was strung together with wires, as if there was a devil in Tempe's body doing torture.

Then Tempe went to the circus; then Mother was guiding her — past the monkeys and the Tasmanian tiger and up to the camel, and there he was. He looked grand, so savage, in leopard-skin drawers, but he would have looked better in a feathered cloak. She walked round him for a while, dreamily, imagining his hair dressed with ornamental combs and greenstone pendants falling from his ears . . . and a necklace of dog's teeth, an ankle-bracelet of shells. But his face was perfect already — no, she didn't think any tattoos. Then the camel-boy winked, and Tempe winked back.

Because Harry was such a long way away, because Mother said as soon as she saw him: *He is one of us*, Tempe knew that she must find him again. Mother pointed out the short cut through the forest, and at

135

its end he stood beside the camel, smiling as if he knew she would come, as if he recognized their likeness, too. She left Ida and Maud to strike up acquaintance with the Spotted Girl and he led her to a tent full of straw. Oh, he was clever — he knew what her body wanted.

Afterwards, he seemed to think an introduction necessary and started to talk. Tempe didn't really listen; she only heard words here and there. She felt disappointed, for somehow he didn't trust her; he must pretend to be someone else. He said he was Edward Thrush — Eddie, and the workman's cottage had been handy to Queen Street, for Dad worked on the wharf.

But it was ridiculous, it was high fantasy, of course, for Tempe knew quite well he wasn't Eddie; that he hadn't lived in a cottage in Auckland — not Queen Street with its carts and horses and cabs, but... Yes, she saw him distinctly — properly primitive, as he waded down-stream, poking here and there with a stick, tossing the slippery eels high up the bank.

Home was all right, Eddie said, but Teacher at school was his enemy. Teacher was too fond of the cane, so Ed took off with the circus... though he missed city life and once the camel bit his hand.

Tempe didn't listen. When his mouth stopped talking she told him how she had been searching and searching, looking for years. She said how important it was that she should find her way back to Mother; how she must remember the old secret language, must remember Mother's name (not Linda, but her real name); must get the words fixed in her head as part of an everyday language, not merely recall them as she played at Lady in the secret pool. "You must help me," Tempe said, and he smiled, he looked bemused. Then suddenly Mother was back, nudging at Tempe's mind, helping her to remember the words from Mr Maufe's book — the book that told about Mount Eden. And: "You are Tane," she said, as if she recited a lesson. "Great Tane — father of all black birds, life-giver, fertilizer, forest god." He laughed at her, then, he was modest. "You can call me anything you like, old love," he said — making her be only a body again. Tempe shut her eyes. "Oh, oh," someone cried from a long way off. "Do you love me?"

Next day the circus moved on. The rickety caravans and the bony horses looked all right from a distance. They made a nursery rhyme frieze going over the hill, and the children of the little town waved and laughed at the camel's wavering hump.

The camel went but Ed Thrush stayed. ("Yes," Tempe said — the Tempe who was only a body — "I will call you Eddie. Anyway, I don't remember the other name. What was it? — who was it you reminded me of?") Ed stayed because Tempe hid him in Mr Maufe's shed that sheltered the brougham and the elegant phaeton that were rarely used. Hiding Ed was an adventure. There was a red blanket to keep him warm, and the adventure was part of a romantic novelette. Yes — Eddie was a soldier wounded in the Franco-Prussian War and Tempe crept in to wipe away the trickles of blood and feed him peaches in brandy.

It was cosy under the blanket, but: "Tempe, Tempe" — always Blanche was calling from the verandah, always everything was spoiled. Tempe had to hurry into her clothes so quickly, so regularly, that each time, because of Blanche's voice, they must be on guard.

Yet Eddie Thrush was no one. He had dirty fingernails. His dad worked on the Queen Street Wharf; Ma Thrush took in washing. But he knew how to satisfy, how to work away the torment in her body; he could reduce Tempe to a voice she hardly knew crooning love words from a distance. But the spell didn't last that long — after a while her voice trailed away and she opened her eyes. Her body felt rested, certainly, but almost any man could have done it.

And then Mother would speak and everything would be transformed. With Mother's voice in her ear, Tempe was a different person. Her body was unimportant; she was Tempe with a mind extended, possessed. And he wasn't Eddie at all: not Ed, but Tane or someone like him.

But your mind swinging this way and that meant your head was in a constant state of flux. Though Tempe didn't remember when he was Eddie that a Tane existed, though she felt the same way about Eddie when he was Tane, there was always a vague sense of muddle. Then, when she started matching Eddie with Harry, the muddle was so badly scrambled that she didn't think she could bear it. She had a headache, a tight band of worry stretched from ear to ear. Then, when she tried consciously to summon up Mother for guidance, she couldn't find her at all. Mother was only Linda who had died — a shadowy figure mixed up with titoki berries and rose petals, a silk dress and Father's wideawake hat.

The Tempe who most certainly owned to a body,

knew she must help herself. Knew that to do so she must choose between Eddie and Harry (if there was Eddie there was no Tane). The fancy ball was coming... Now that would provide the perfect backdrop against which to choose. Harry, however, was nowhere near (being far from The Peach Groves, with Cissie at Epsom). But a word in Augustus's ear might remedy that, one good turn deserving another. "Oh please, dear Mr Maufe," Tempe might lisp, suitably little-girlish, "if you can tempt Harry here, I will do all I can to place Heart's Desire in your path."

⁕

New Zealand, even Mr Maufe's part, kept being different to what Ida expected. In the beginning there were only Uncle's letters to go by. Mama's voice read sentences aloud, and you saw the gumfield and his red flannel shirt distinctly. That was the first New Zealand — Uncle in his red shirt and moleskins, leaning on his spade. Then there were lessons at the nursery table, and the geographical reader made New Zealand stranger. Smoke came out of the ground and a little greenstone man was lucky. "We will go there some day," Ida promised Queechy. There, you'd never wear gloves or stockings or all the other horrid things. You'd wander in the forest barefoot, and your hair would be bleached of all its ginger — in New Zealand, Ida would be as rose-petal pretty as Maud.

Not true, though. For they had come to the dreamland and behind Uncle's house there was forest. Ida had been there, but she'd worn stockings —

139

it had been Tempe who had played at Eve. And Auntie's garden was mostly English and the Epsom dessert plates were the same as those at home. Oh yes, it was a different New Zealand to the one she'd expected, certainly, but Ida wasn't disappointed. It was worth wearing the gloves, and still having freckles, if there was Tempe and Uncle to watch. And Mr Maufe. And the nasty expression in Auntie's eyes when she looked at Tempe. And the sad one in Mama's when she looked at Uncle.

But, at the same time, that other more foreign New Zealand stayed something you hoped you'd find. When Mr Maufe proffered his invite it seemed that Ida would actually get there. "Hot springs," he had said, "and peaches and tree-ferns as well." He hadn't lied, though they hadn't visited Te Aroha yet to investigate the baths. Some day soon, though, assured Mama but Ida didn't very much care. For things were different, different. The tree-ferns and all the rest of the forest couldn't be faulted — Ida couldn't have dreamed up anything better. And the peaches had fallen into the grass with a lovely muffled thud; you picked one up and there was a gruesome bruise and countless scurrying ants. Perfect, perfect. So many peaches to eat, so fat and free-stone that soon you scorned them. And there were humps of jewel-green moss and little amber-winged moths, and the tea-tree bush in flower look-ed just like a big white cloud.

But Ida didn't care. For New Zealand, now, didn't mean aspects of a landscape, however natural or the reverse. New Zealand, to Ida at The Peach Groves, meant people more than ever — not savages with tattooed faces but the same people she'd

watched at Epsom, with Auntie and Uncle subtracted, with the addition of several more Maufes
and a camel-boy from a circus. Usually people were
boring. You felt most of them were meant for
Mama and Papa, Uncle and Auntie from the day
they were born. You suspected that they might
come alive most of all when alone at last, propriety's
well-marked path petered out, they tripped into the
last little bit of dying that proved the most vivid
part of living a life.

But New Zealand, and now The Peach Groves,
had turned everything topsy-turvy. The heroes and
villains had got free of the story-book and stalked
the drawing-room carpet. All the old certitudes
meant nothing. Under the layers of elegant clothes
were bodies that lusted and cried in the night. An
uncle could still be a man who was worthless . . .
and not Mama, but a matron with a mouth that
pouted to be kissed; not Auntie, but the little match
girl, crying to come in from the cold. Everything
and everyone had turned so different that Ida was
glad she had Queechy. For, without the doll and
that WORTHLESS cross-stitched to her stomach,
Ida might have felt afraid. Illogically, embroidered
on to calico, Uncle's opinion of himself turned into
a joke that took the sting from all the secrets Ida
tracked.

The very air felt laced with them. Ida felt a pattern evolving. Everyone seemed caught up in it
except herself and Papa, sitting safe in his armchair
across the Tasman.

Though, of course, Papa did more than sit. He
was a lawyer who walked about, and ran up the
steps of the General Post Office to send off a weekly

letter to Mama. But somehow Ida saw him sitting. In her head everyone was neatly labelled, everyone had their pose. Papa sat cosy before the fire (even though it was summer) and waited for their return. Mama stood facing Uncle Harry in her dress with the low-cut neck. Uncle snuggled against Tempe's cheek, but looked over her shoulder at Mama . . . Oh yes, Ida saw them all: Aunt Cissie, Maud, Mr Maufe . . .

And seeing, imagining, Ida couldn't help but shiver. For, despite Queechy and the stitching on her stomach, it would be easy to feel afraid. Only now and then, of course. When Mr Maufe edged that little bit closer. When Zillah's *Take care* was more urgent. Imagining, Ida sometimes felt resentful. For it wasn't fair. Sometimes she didn't feel like a child at all. It seemed as if New Zealand had turned her into someone other than herself. Often, she felt more grown-up than all the rest of them. Watching them play out their secrets, sensing a pattern evolving, she felt as though she was somehow related to God.

But Ida was still child enough to get excited when Mr Maufe announced one evening that, instead of their usual concert, they'd fill the gap between dinner and bedtime with a programme of parlour games.

At first it was fun. They started off with Dumb Crambo and then Miss Queenie Maufe provided them each with a wine-glass and spoon and Mama sat down at the piano and vamped out an air and when Mr Maufe cried "Spoons" each glass was tapped on its edge, thus producing an accompaniment of spoon music to good effect.

But after a sip of raisin wine the amusements took a turn for the worst. Miss Ethel Maufe thought a Spelling-bee would be improving as well as enjoyable, and so they must puzzle over such horrors as "phthisical" and "dithyrambic".

But the Dwarf was very much worse. Mr Maufe stage-managed the wonderful phenomenon, and for a while it seemed it might have to be cancelled, for Octavius tried to escape. At first Ida thought him as much a spoil-sport as everyone else. "Oh please, Oc," she cried with all the others, "don't be mean, don't ruin the fun." Their wheedling voices tempted him back; Octavius took his hand off the drawing-room door-knob and went behind the sheet that did for a curtain. Tempe went, too, at Mr Maufe's bidding and there were a series of bumps and scuffles before their host came forward, very formal, to introduce himself as Exhibitor. The exhibit was his little friend, Count Borowlaski. The Count, according to Mr Maufe, was a Polish dwarf, so small that when he was taken to church to be christened his mother made a bed for him in her shoe.

When the sheet was drawn back it really did seem that there was a stanger in their midst. The Count was good enough for the circus. He stood on a table before them, quite the most comical little fellow Ida had seen. But his head was so large . . . but his head belonged to Octavius. Behind Ida someone started crying, and then Mrs Maufe stumbled from the room. Mama giggled nervously; Miss Ethel Maufe began biting her nails. Everyone looked uncomfortable except Mr Maufe. He smiled his dear old man's grin fiercer than ever; he kept on talking. The

Count, he said with a snigger, was remarkable for his intelligence and wit. He was also most highly accomplished: he played on the guitar proficiently, he could dance. And here Mr Maufe gave the Dwarf's legs a poke with a sharp little stick, and obediently the Count's feet stirred.

It was awful watching Oc do it. For it was Octavius, without doubt, who played Dwarf with a small degree of help from Tempe. The Count's feet were the hands of Octavius, the Count's head was Oc's as well. The Count's fingers were provided by Tempe, who managed to hide herself while she thrust her hands over Oc's shoulders. Stockings and shoes had been put on those artificial feet, and the Count wore a child's pinafore, as well, to hide the comical way in which the portions of his two creators were united.

It was funny, of course; and clever how the table-cloth hid every part of Oc below waist. And Mr Maufe improvised such nonsense, and his stick poked so well that now the Count's dance-steps had turned quite sprightly. Mrs Maufe was merely eccentric — her sobs didn't signify much. Now Miss Ethel laughed as loud as Mama — Oh yes, Papa was most marvellously witty; oh yes, wasn't Octavius perfectly darling, wasn't his head a scream? Everyone laughed and laughed; the exhibition was voted a success. As long as you didn't look into Count Borowlaski's eyes. For Octavius's eyes were full of tears. Oh, he was funny; oh, didn't his head look more lolling and stupid than usual. Maud was in fits, but Ida couldn't bear to look.

They recovered with more raisin wine, and then Mr Maufe proposed a game of hide-and-seek as finishing touch to the evening. He would be seeker and off they must go — one-two-three . . . on count of ten, coming ready or not.

Ida and Maud held hands and sped up the stairs. "Quickly," urged Ida, "find somewhere safe." For it was important that they should escape him. She couldn't bear the thought of his old hands hunting them out. "Oh hurry, hurry," moaned Ida, for he would be after them, she knew for sure.

And first they ran into Miss Ethel's room, but the stink of zinc cream drove them away. "In here," hissed Maud, and the next room, embowered in William Morris olive leaves, belonged to Miss Queenie. Holding their breath, turned into statues, they sank down behind an ornamental armchair that resembled a bishop's canopied throne. Just in time. For he came in, he was panting, and the first place he looked was in the wardrobe, and then he tried under the bed. "Oh please, dear God," prayed Ida. "Oh please, dear Queechy . . ." Perhaps praying did the trick, for then he went out, then they heard him searching the attics.

Downstairs was surely safer — Mama was some-where there. Down they ran, and then blindly through a doorway. Ida went in first and Maud followed. It was only Maud that Tempe, skulking in the hall's shadows, spied. Pretty little Maud, the image of her mama — and one good turn deserved another . . .

The room turned out to be Mr Maufe's study. There were rows of tatty books, but there didn't seem to be anywhere to hide.

Then the door-knob was turning — then there was no time left at all. Automatically, Ida crawled beneath the chenille tablecloth's bobbles, but Maud didn't follow.

It wasn't a game any more. It had never been one and, really, she had known all along. For Maud wanted him to pounce. She would stand there so still, she would do anything he wanted. A little flush crept over her body and she felt sweetly sticky, too; it felt as if her body sweated peach juice. She shut her eyes and stood there, and then silently he was upon her. At first his hands were gentle.

Augustus loved her so much. He knew he could never hurt her. It was like worshipping. He shut his eyes the same as she, and it was as if they played a static game of Blind-man's-buff. Little angel, little pale girl. His fingers fondled her hair, his mouth grazed her cheek. Never ever would he hurt her. His fingers lingered at the neck of her dress. Which was when she flinched. Which was what did it — caused the feeling of content to fade, made the loving hatred come strong. For she wasn't an angel at all: Young Apollo had died years ago. His fingers tightened on her throat and she whimpered. His eyes were open now — he saw her. She was only flesh and blood, she would cheat him like everything else. Did he want to keep her from growing up? — of course.

Under the table Ida heard Maud whimper, and then she stopped being afraid. She crawled out, but she was so quick that it felt as if she flew. She leapt at his back, as the deliverer always did. He was a villain and he toppled; her weight pulled him down and they lay tangled together on the carpet. Everything happened at once. They fell, and Maud came free. But not in the way Ida had hoped, for Maud had started to laugh. She rubbed at her neck as if it was sore, but she laughed as much as she had when Oc had been Dwarf.

Then Tempe was in the study, too. Then Miss Queenie and Miss Ethel and Octavius. Mrs Maufe came next; Mama was last. Only Mrs Maufe and Octavius showed concern. Ida waited for Maud to tell. It would be lovely to see him taken away. What happened to dirty old men? Would the thrashing be hard enough?

But Maud's mouth was fixed in a smile. It was as if nothing bad had happened at all; as if it had only been that game of hidey, and here they both were — tagged at last.

Ida knew the telling must come from herself. But for an instant she hesitated, and then it was too late. The terror had inched artfully away. Maud smiled, and the grown-ups clustered round and the room was full of soft breathing. The sun would certainly shine tomorrow; surely no one could hurt you. But Ida's mind remembered coldly. She hated him and his innocent Santa Claus pose.

Mr Maufe was on his feet again. He smoothed down his jacket and twitched at his neck-tie. His dear old face was beaming. He said that the naughty chicks had given him an excellent run for his money. He said they deserved a half-crown each. His hand trembled as he held out the bribing coins, and the grown-ups murmured approvingly, Mama's eyes said you had to accept. Ida took hers scornfully; Maud smiled sweeter than ever. And then Mama shooed them off to bed.

147

4

The sea subtracted, the river in its place, it was almost the same summer here, as at Glenelg. Though not so hot; though a milder shade of blue above. But if you left out the unsettling native part — the tree-ferns and lavatory leaves and all the other bits of bush with trickier names — New Zealand stopped being foreign; if you concentrated on the Maufes' garden you were reassured. Although you'd travelled so far you could still be surrounded by England transplanted; though at Glenelg, and now here at The Peach Groves, the peaches and passionfruit, the tomatoes and geraniums had come out into the open — a conservatory not being deemed essential for their welfare.

Summer was Maud's favourite season. Often her mind would stop neatly labelling and worrying over such pressing matters as the style of her latest dress, and she'd wander in the garden — her favourite summer place, and be overwhelmed by a multitude of sights and sounds and smells and touchings.

For, despite not often indulging in flights of fancy, Maud regularly gave in to feeling. Rather than bother to imagine yourself as a rose, it was more pleasant to sniff up the scent of the real ones, to poke your finger into their tasselled centres and stroke their veined petals — till you were startled by something ugly: a beetle playing bogey-man at the rose's heart. Or she'd throw herself down on the lawn and, for once unmindful of the state of her dress, feel the teasing prick of countless grass blades and the sharp bite of ants. Not bothering to think was beautiful. Soft winds lapped her skin and the papery hibiscus flowers, hot pink on the bush, had nothing to do with those sad furled things lying faded on the grass beneath them.

Though she wouldn't have recognized the word, Maud had been a sensualist from birth. Having a body was reason enough for living; particularly now, when her body had never seemed so precious. Oh you are beautiful, Maud whispered to herself at night — though, really, it was as if she said the words to another. For she admired her body dispassionately; she was George's daughter as well as Blanche's: sensuality was laced refreshingly with cool strands of logic. Detachment was easy for, as well, Maud had been brought up properly, according to Adelaide upper-class standards. It didn't seem strange that the thing you valued so highly should be treated as something unseemly — an unmentionable wished away beneath a variety of starched and pin-tucked layers before it was lady-like laced out of shape. Then, too, Parson's voice warned of Hell-fire with relish each Sunday. And, though part of her shivered deliciously at the thought of those flames on her flesh, the practical side of Maud knew when it was prudent to sidestep. Of course, you got an extra thrill from pretending, so that early on it became habitual to keep her eyes lowered, to wear her lips in a way that suggested she perpetually sucked on a ju-jube. "An angel child," the grown-ups pronounced and Mama looked proud. Because she did, Maud would pretend for ever. Mama's approval was the sweetest thing in the world, the reward that meant most. For Mama, Maud would have willed her body to die.

Because of loving Blanche so much, there was extra reason for Maud to keep the intensity of her feelings for the garden and summer and her body a secret. Mama, who was always so perfectly composed, would never understand.

Calmly, good-girl Maud saw her future stretching ahead. For Mama, she'd relinquish passionfruit seeds and peaches, and stick to less messy fruits and a dip in a finger-bowl after. She'd stop feeling. Summer would be merely a season that meant ants in the sugar and sweat-shields sewn into your dresses. The hibiscus would thrust its tongue at the sky, ignored; for hubba there'd be someone the same as Papa, and then a series of happy events. Loving Mama, how else could life be?

And yet there was Mr Maufe. His hands were comforting. They were gentleman's hands, kind and soothing, never too busy to spare Master Bob a touch. It was only natural that she should appreciate their feel. Nothing was wrong . . .

Liar. You'd known from the start. Mr Maufe wasn't good at all. He was evil and you shouldn't touch his book. But you had to, you couldn't stop looking.

At The Peach Groves, each day was an adventure. His hands might touch her just that little bit longer; he might put another book in her way. Maud was always looking in mirrors — how could he resist her?

He was a bad old man but she was only a little girl. Pretending was Maud's forte; she could always skip back. Papa's cash and Mama's class and the wealth of eyelet embroidery on her petticoat guaranteed that. And he was a gentleman, after all. Truly, they'd never do anything really wrong.

So it was merely a game of hidey when he chased her all over the house. Trapped in his study at last, watch-dog Ida gone under the table, Maud waited for him to come. She stayed calm, even when he found her. But then Maud shivered with excitement and everything changed. For his hand tightened and suddenly it was ridiculous — what he did seemed real and she started to fight him.

But the danger only lasted for an instant. Safe again, Maud turned stupid and went back to believing herself immune and, without meaning to, began to laugh. Oh, it was funny — the expression on his face when Ida made her attack.

Maud laughed so much that, laughing, she almost felt frightened. For once, things seemed to have escaped her control.

❀

Zillah didn't always scare you. Lately, up in the box-room, her pen had progressed at a more

151

leisured pace and, instead of worrying over little lost girls, Ida was entertained by the Queen of the Gipsies and the Priestess of Folly as they came to life on Zillah's page.

For even a visionary artist couldn't resist it. The fancy ball was drawing closer and The Peach Groves buzzed with excitement. The dressing-up box was regularly rummaged; each evening, now, instead of making music or partaking of parlour games, everyone retired early to plan their costumes.

Mama, to begin with, couldn't decide between Arctic Maiden or Elaine from *Idylls of the King.* She saw herself perfectly as the latter, a band of stars circling her brow, a lily in one hand and Lancelot's letter in the other. But Maud was set on the former and why should Blanche disappoint her? — besides which, while she had nothing suitable for that gown of rich gold that Elaine deserved, she owned just the outfit for the frosty maid. Her white tulle would suit admirably, with the addition of several talc cloth tongues to imitate icicles. She'd carry a fan painted with a snow scene and a flight of robins; her hair should hang loose, and be covered with frosting powder and a veil sewn with swansdown tufts.

Mama disposed of, Maud pondered over a costume for herself and Ida. Sisters desiring to appear in garb which assimilated, might choose Music and Painting, or Salt and Fresh Water, or the Roses of York and Lancaster. Ida lacking suggestions, the Roses seemed best. They possessed the requisite white dresses; all that was needed was a quantity of red and white blooms from The Peach Groves' garden.

And Tempe would attend as Undine, in Nile-green crêpe looped with waterlilies and grasses as befitted one who ruled o'er lakes and rivers. Ethel, as Grace Darling, plumped for red and white wool . . . and she rather thought a life-buoy fastened to her back, a small lighthouse and anchor as chatelaine; ropes round the waist, a lighted lantern in the hand, a fishing-net on her shoulder. Queenie, not caring for decided fancy dress, had settled on a fashion of the hour and would get herself up as a Nocturne, which meant stylish black and white, after Whistler. And Oc would be Harlequin; Mr Maufe, Mephistopheles; Mrs Maufe, The Trailing Garments of The Night.

In the box-room, Zillah would draw for a bit, then take up her needle to sew. It didn't seem to matter that the light was dim — her needle seemed to know its path. In their snug retreat from the world of light, Ida watched Night's costume develop. Already there was an inky bodice and a pair of long pendant sleeves; now Zillah had started stitching at a skirt flecked with silver stars. Soon more stars and a dashing of comets would spangle a satin train, while a scarf of pale gauze would represent the Milky Way.

Zillah talked as she sewed, and Ida felt confused. For now her friend couldn't be neatly divided into two: Zillah in the box-room; Wifey downstairs. Beause of fancy ball anticipation, things were muddled. One minute it was Zillah who, snipping at tinsel thread, prattled childishly, excitedly: Would there be conjurors or Christy Minstrels during the breaks from dancing? Did Ida think there'd be a Fairy Pool to fish in for presents? . . . Then it

153

was Wifey who reminisced of all the fancy balls that were part of her past. Ida sighed enviously. Things had been arranged differently once. It hardly seemed possible that such fine young *beaux* as the Boiled Bull-dog's should have existed — all those French and English officers (and all such nice fellows, too). "And of course," Wifey remembered fondly, "the girls ran after me proportionately . . ." They used to circle her like a flock of doves. "And did love me so."

It was interesting to learn that Wifey's grandmama had danced at balls held at Carlisle House, Soho, where Ladies Waldegrave and Pembroke and the Duchess of Hamilton were among the beauties. And fancy, that when the crinoline was the mode, even peasant dress was slightly distended . . . "Though now, during the reign of the Jersey," Wifey continued knowingly, "elastic silk serves for the bodices of Gipsy, Folly and many others. And tulle has almost entirely superseded tarlatan."

Already the fancy ball had worked wonders. Up in the box-room Zillah turned into a Wifey as silly as a normal grown-up. Downstairs, Mr Maufe was merely a harmless old man, a genial host, as he worried over weather, moon, champagne and every other particular and hoped two upstanding feathers would do for Mephistopheles's horns.

Ida relaxed. Surely the worst was over. After the ball they'd sample the waters at Te Aroha — and then back to Epsom for a brief ta-ta to Auntie and Uncle, and on to Glenelg and Papa. And, without meaning to, she felt disappointed. For, despite Mr Maufe's try in the study, nothing absolutely awful had happened; New Zealand was tame after all.

The first thing she'd do when she got home would be to unpick that cross-stitch blemish from Queechy's stomach.

And then it was the morning before the evening and Cook and the maids worked like mad. The kitchen was a magic place and Ida couldn't keep away. The triangular sandwiches looked like folded-up hankies; there were harlequin-coloured little cakes and a great big chocolate one and a snow cake with coconut trim. The *pièce de résistance* was a fairy castle of rout-cakes, encircled by a tremulous trifle sea and a wall of *meringues à la crème*.

Strangers came with fragile gold chairs and though there were innumerable flowers in the garden, extra ones were sent from town. The drawing-room furniture disappeared and the Turkey carpet went under a drugget; doors kept banging, the piano was tuned.

When everything was ready — the dance cards and the little pencils (blue for gentlemen, pink for ladies) arranged in the straw basket on the bamboo table, the rout-cake castle set in place of honour in the supper-room, the music book on the piano open at "The Gorilla Quadrille" (for Queenie was up to date, and knew of the vogue for gorillas in London) — Ida and Maud were led away by Mama for a session of hair washing.

It hurt when she pulled the comb through the squeaky wet tangles, it was worse when she plaited tightly, but the resultant braids were surely worth that tug at the temples. You'd bear the pain smiling, for, because of it, you'd end up with the desired degree of fancy ball frizz.

As they walked in the garden to dry their hair,

they gathered York and Lancaster's roses. Then, inside again, they must rest on their beds. Tonight they'd stay up later than ever before.

When Ida woke, the afternoon had faded away. Night was almost arrived and the house stirred welcomingly, it was alive with gossipy whispers. Somewhere a bell rang silverly and there was a low rippling laugh and then a sharp little sound as if someone stamped a ladylike foot. Through the window a daffodil moon swam above the stables and, leaning out, Ida saw a wavering line of smaller moons beneath it, for the trees along the drive burned with lanterns. Even if you shut your eyes you knew that something special was near. Excitement had crept into everything. The crickets had never shrilled so brightly; there was a fresh smell, as if the garden had just been watered . . . Ida opened her eyes and two figures, naked as statues, tangled on the lawn; then lay still as swimmers becalmed; then were washed away by darker night.

It had been Tempe and someone . . . it had been no one at all, only Ida's eyes playing a trick. But Tempe and who? — then Ida stopped puzzling, for Mama came in with the lamp.

She undid their braids (the frizz was perfect) and then they were allowed to watch while she turned into Arctic Maid. The best part was when she powdered her hair, and first had to dampen it with starch and then shake the frosting well over. But when she had her dress on and the veil with its dabs of snowy down, they weren't allowed to touch her. She was like a frosty stranger with her spangled hair and the talc cloth icicles, the glittering loops of crystal fringe.

5

And through the night a strange company proceeds: Joan of Arc and the Queen of the Butterflies, Dick Turpin and the Tall Gamekeeper in *Pickwick*. At home they are but Mama and Papa, Uncle and Aunt, dear Bro', sweet Sis; but, Peach Groves bound, fancy costume has given them leave for a little while to play out their dreams. This puritan Papa wears a looking-glass inset on each toe-cap, for the improper purpose of peeping up skirts; that angel Mama has all the names of past lovers embroidered to her prunella boot-tops.

For most, it is an easy journeying. There is a coachman to confront the darkness; the steady drumming of hoof-beats is comforting. Accordingly, Desdemona smooths her silver-cloth stomacher placidly; a Gentleman of Olden Time eases off a buckled shoe.

But there are those who travel harder — Amazons who ride in from outlying districts, costumes strapped to saddles in small parcels; young bloods who follow a forest path on heavily booted foot (their dancing pumps are in their pockets). There is one who has been travelling all day — now it is night and he is on the river at last . . . his boat skims on, under the willows; at the landing-stage the waggonette waits. There is another, whose journey has merely taken him across the lawn — he has reached the front door, now, this swarthy Fairy Prince in ruby velvet doublet (the dressing-up box has served Ed well).

The house is marvellously changed. It doesn't matter, now, about the fake bricks and the tortuous fretwork. It is an overgrown doll's house on the outside, only; once past the door The Peach Groves lives up to its name — even Oc's imaginings could not improve it.

Everywhere there are quivering candles and accordion-pleated Chinese lanterns: the ballroom glows pinkish-gold. There are masses of flowers; ropes of ivy and asparagus fern garland the walls. In the supper-room there are rose-buds in crystal vases.

To begin with, Arctic Maiden and the Roses of York and Lancaster, Undine and Grace Darling and a Nocturne, Harlequin and Mephistopheles and The Trailing Garments of The Night were the only ones there.

And Tempe was angry because Arctic Maid's neck-line was cut lower than Undine's (. . . and will he really come? Will I know which one I should choose when I see them together? Which one? — but, oh, it was good what we did in the grass . . . the lanterns like big oranges overhead, and the grass with the same smell as cut flower-stalks) . . . Mephistopheles worried even worse. He was sure the red velvet was a mistake. He lacked the swagger to live up to its devilishness; his calves in silk hose bulged with veins. His horns drooped sadly, for he would never do it — never regain Young Apollo, or put that strangle-hold on little white girl... Who is willing, though he doesn't know it; though she doesn't know what it is she wills. For Maud, there is still a mystery — the beast's snarling muzzle is veiled in cheating gauze. For Maud, dreams still come true; shamrock sprigs bestow luck, without doubt; the Language of Flowers assures the rose to be a sign of joy and love, and innocence to shine in the lily's bell (even though pennyroyal's message is "Flee away", and the nettle signifies cruelty and creeping cerberus, horror)... Oc chose Harlequin because of the mask. It was black and silky, so smooth; there were slits for his eyes. Masked, he felt himself hidden; he was safe, with a standard size head. His feet felt light and his body, graceful; his slippers were pointed, and he admired them as he practised a dance step. He was so close to her; she'd be his partner for Sir Roger de Coverley. Happy, Oc wasn't sure who he meant; Mama was beside him, so was Maud: he loved them both... She was beautiful. Beauty had crawled in at her mouth like a woolly caterpillar; like a wavering ant it entered her ear. It was the daddy-long-legs that crept up her leg, the velvet moth that fondled her arm. But no — silly Zillah was at it again. Dreaming, saying her nonsense. She wasn't Zillah Whiffin, she hadn't listened as coffins were hammered — no, never; not Zillah, not the Boiled B. I am Mrs Augustus Maufe, she told herself, wonderingly. Mrs Maufe, made beautiful by Night's trailing dress. There were that many stars on the skirt, though in the end her eyes had deceived her, for some of them were sewn on crooked. And beautiful, star-spangled, Mrs Maufe adjusted the gauze scarf that meant the Milky Way. Then she took Oc's hand and betrayed The Trailing Garments of The Night, for then she was only Mama . . . And once she had been Little Princess, getting *The Globe Alphabet* to heart. You started at *A* which stood for "Anchor", you finished at *Z* for "Zebra". And in between were the ones that had ruined her life: "*N* stands for a Nabob, a lord of the East, who likes on strong coffee and sweetmeats to feast" and: "*U* stands for the Uniform, in which are seen the soldiers who fight for their country and Queen". Little Princess was as door-nail dead as Fred, but, Nocturnally-clad, Queenie couldn't get the silly rhymes out of her mind: "*T* stands for the Tiger, a terrible beast, that lives in the jungles and woods of the East", etcetera . . . Ethel was a heroine at last, but she hadn't thought it would be so uncomfy. The rolled-up sleeves chafed her, the sailor's tasselled cap didn't suit, all the accessories weighed her down. As Grace Darling, how would she dance? More to the point, who would ask her? . . . Blanche looked haughtier, more Snow Queen perfect than ever, but how lonely it was to be alone. When had Harry begun wanting to be safe, how could he prefer Cissie and Home? For an instant Blanche wanted to cry, but then Arctic Maiden tossed her silvery head. He would never know, but she would show him. She would dance and dance . . . Red rose, petals curling under to form fat velvet cushions — veined velvet, shading from red to near black. Sniffing up the scent of Lancaster's roses — an ideal occupation, for at the same time, little-girl innocent, you peeped. You watched every one of them, you waited for high jinks to start; for the powder to melt off those beautiful faces, for the red mouths to bleed away. Spit-beads and patches of sweat would appear; there'd be wine stains and cake crumbs, ripped arm-holes and the rending of seams. Lovely, lovely, and Ida sniffed harder and the aphis hugged the rose's heart. Then the door-bell rang and the fancy ball started beginning . . .

Usually reality disappointed; most times it was safest to dream. But tonight anticipation didn't lead on to a let-down — the fancy ball was in progress and there was nothing to fault.

The room was full of light; it was a perfect room, welcoming, it glowed like the warm pink inside of the sea-shell you held to your ear. The music was perfect, too. The pianist's fingers were prancing ponies; oh, they skipped nimbly, so gay; then *Z-i-n-g* . . . — all the silvery high notes plunged to meet thundering low ones, and the pianist's hand was a white fish, plummeting waterfall-downwards, and the ponies had pranced away. Now the music was slow and throbbing, and you saw the dancers properly. They were like magic; so wonderful, that it wasn't necessary to like or dislike them (and while you puzzled for an opinion cause the magic to fade). Charms and chatelaines and cockades, fans and feathers and frisettes, patches and plumes, tiaras and tridents . . . — they were all here. But the faces were the most perfect things. Even the ugly ones were marvellously bold. For once there was nothing feeble; hunchbacks and port-wine birthmarks were worn proudly.

Now the slow waltz had ended and a Quadrille of All Nations was announced. Not everyone took part. If you hadn't chosen to be a Canadian Snowwreath, or something equally patriotic, you merely watched. Ida had to leave the pianist then, for red rose and white meant England. They were in with John Bull and the Vicar of Wakefield, while over there was a Rhenish Peasant and, a bit further off, the Fair Maid of Perth.

You danced and the room danced, too. You ceased caring about your roses and, as you dipped and wove and tossed your crinkled hair, petals came loose to be crushed underfoot. The rose petals fell; the room was bathed in light. Outside was the night, but velvet curtains kept it at bay. One by one the dances on your card came up. The Trailing Garments of The Night snored in a corner while Harlequin clasped the Rose of York's waist and whirled her round the room.

Ida was content to sit and watch. As well as Harlequin, there were two other masked ones. One was a Fairy Prince in ruby, with a feather in his cap and a leopard skin over his shoulder; the other, all in black, might be a bearded Hamlet. Both of them had danced with Undine . . .

Then Ida must have fallen asleep, for when she looked again, everything was changed. The miniature pencils had crossed off several more dances; they were up to the Supper Dance and, in the supper-room, maids in fig-leaf aprons were running about and the rout-cake castle looked so nice — who'd believe that it would soon be despoiled?

Ida stationed herself before the chocolate cake, for that was the refreshment she fancied most. There was a furry taste in her mouth and her brain felt pickled (decidedly, she must have slept). Which was why, perhaps, when the music died away and the dancers came trooping in, she saw them strangely.

How they jostled; how — beautiful, perfectly ugly — they pushed their bodies forward. Ida was trapped on a chocolate mouthful. Their bodies leaned over her, spilling breasts and beauty-spots, pearl necklaces and tickling fichus. Now she was pinned by a Cavalier's arm as he plundered the dish of cold fowl. Lace fell from his elegant wrist into the sauce boat; he made an awful noise munching, his lips were slippery.

Ida ducked and made her escape, and felt more confused than ever. For two of the strangers were curiously familiar. Hamlet and the Fairy Prince — who were they, didn't she know them? And, suddenly, staring at the Prince she recognized him. It was the leopard skin that did it — that, and his tan. He was the camel-boy from the circus, of course . . . Easy, really. But who, then, was Hamlet?

Ida side-stepped the problem neatly, by letting sleep claim her. Next thing she knew, she was lying in bed. The piano sounded faintly from downstairs, which meant that the ball still progressed, though Ida and Maud hadn't lasted the evening. They lay in bed, and Mama bent over them. She was still there when Ida gave in again to sleep.

But when she woke at first light, another had

taken her place. Tempe hung over the bed. It had been she, then, who'd been shaking — shaking Ida's shoulder, forcing her out of sleep. Maud was sitting up already, rubbing her eyes.

Tempe still wore her fancy costume. There was an awful determination about her. You knew straight away that the worst thing of all had happened. Perhaps The Peach Groves was burning and she'd come to save them; perhaps a flood as bad as Noah's approached.

Tempe made them get out of bed. She didn't even give them time to put on their wrappers, but hustled them down the stairs, down into the kitchen, and out through the kitchen door. The bushes in the herb garden were full of delicious smells, but she didn't even allow them to pinch with their fingers, but hurried them round the side of the house.

The lawn was drenched with dew — your toes sank right in, they felt cool and nice. Tired and bewildered as Ida was, she knew she'd never forget the wonder of being out so early. She'd remember the feel of the grass and the queer greeny light. The sun was on its way up, yet the moon still hovered, a mother-of-pearl button in the sky. Little winds blew; the garden looked fresh and jewel-like, set about with the darker tones of the bush. A lizard darted across their path; first birds began to call. The lanterns glowed palely in the trees along the drive.

If only the house hadn't been there. If only it might have shrunk as small as the doll's house it resembled . . . shrunk smaller, till the sham bricks and barley-sugar columns and hideous fretwork had disappeared entirely. It was all the fault of the house. What Tempe led them to see had nothing to do with the morning.

But, at first, what they saw was beautiful. Tempe led them on to the verandah, she took them up to a window: Through it they saw this beautiful thing. It was like looking through the door of the Catholic church. Tempe pushed them closer to the pane, so that Ida's nose felt as squashed as a koala's. "Look," spat Tempe. "See them," and the room was all golden, the room through the window was a chapel. The gold chairs made a magic circle and if you stepped inside you were enchanted. They lay on a heap of cushions, they were like saints. So pale — like the lady and gentleman asleep on the tomb, and he'd been in the Crusades and the history book didn't tell, but you knew they'd always been good and had never done wrong. Tempe made the little girls look. Round them was a bank of flowers. They'd gathered up all the vases — the big ones full of plumed grass and the yellow iris that meant flame of love, and the small crystal ones from the supper-room. There were candles, as well, and they'd looped the garlands of asparagus fern and ivy round and round, so that they were ringed by a ruffled green snake. There were fallen petals and the Chinese lanterns, and: "Look," commanded Tempe, and her hands felt like iron and you had to look, had to see them. But they were statues, pale and washed clean, they did no wrong. They were only lying down, resting together; it was like being Adam and Eve. She was so white, he had sunburned patches. Her frosted hair spread out like a fan; his hair was black, and there were smaller hairs in strange places. They had folded up their fancy costumes, neatly. That was a naked man. It was Uncle Harry, it was Mama.

Tempe jerked Maud's head up, so that she had to look — Maud was crying. Ida had looked all along, it was interesting. All along she had seen: not Arctic Maiden and Hamlet, but Mama and Uncle Harry. They were lying so still that they might have been dead. And then he kissed her again; their bodies came alive, and behind the little girls Tempe was smiling.

Smiling, she loosened her grip and that gave Maud her chance. Ida stood fascinated at the window, but Maud darted under Tempe's arm, and then she was running across the lawn, then the bush had swallowed her up.

6

There had been a ball. Wifey had dressed up to meet it. Night's Trailing Garments had been a credit all round. Mephistopheles had smiled approvingly as they passed in the waltz. Now he lay beside her, snoring gently; beside him, Wifey couldn't sleep.

Her head was full of whirling figures. It was the fault of seeing strangers so rarely. Last night countless numbers had marched on the house, there were strangers in every room.

It had been agreeable watching the dancing, but then Wifey's head hurt so she had to go out to the garden. She'd begun feeling muddled; she knew that Zillah would get her again. And that the spirit guide would get her even worse — would creep in at her finger and make her take up her visionary pen, even though she didn't want to. There was no fun in drawing. Only the pain in your head — then nothing of Wifey left at all; only Zillah and the images falling inky off the nib.

Up in the sky was a big full moon. Wifey lay

down on the grass to watch it, and some of the strangers started leaving. Zillah (for it was she, now, who wore Wifey's body) crouched behind the hawthorn-tree and watched the invaders depart. It was morning but the moon was still there, and where had the bees gone and the stiff-legged grasshopper? The buggies jingled away . . . Goodbye: no more piano, now; feet crunching on gravel. It wasn't pleasant saying ta-ta, for they held out their cheeks to be kissed. Oh men were awful — and he had come all the way in a boat and his black velvet arms reached out for her; she melted into them and his mask lay over his face but she pulled it away. They were brother and sister, and he reckoned she was the only one he had ever wanted; he didn't care if he ended in Hell. And: How I want you, she cried, but: Wait, he said, soppy. We must make it beautiful, he said, and he fetched all the flowers and the cushions from Wifey's sofa. Then it was filthy, and why should Zillah make Wifey watch? Because of being weak she won. Sobbing, she pulled herself up from the grass, and kept her head down so the moon couldn't catch her, and ran inside. She didn't, couldn't, never did remember. She was Wifey (I am, yes, I am). She took off Night's dress and got into bed and tried to match her snores to Hubby's.

But Wifey couldn't sleep. Zillah kept nudging her brain; the spirit guide was an itch in her fingers. At last it was too bad to bear: she went up to the box-room and started to draw. This time the thicket of ink lines that sprang off her pen was thornier, mazier, more dangerous than ever before.

※

She runs and runs. Into the dark heart of the forest. She will run and run, without respite, till in the end she finds Papa and Home.

Home: the cricket that chirped by the kitchen door, and the other one — smaller-voiced, though as persistent — that sounded from the candle-pine in the garden. Home, home: Papa holding out his safe lawyer hands and Boson leaping forward. Oh yes, Maud ran for that — and tea-time and clean white sheets and all the other certitudes: wash-day Monday when the blue-bag tinted the water; Tuesday, when spit sizzled on the iron to test its heat, and a servant fist pressed on to Wednesday that meant a new supply of butterfly cakes and rockies with an almond on top. Thursday was when they did the bedrooms; Friday meant Brasso on a rag . . . Saturday, Sunday — the week passed along so easy.

At home a proper order reigned. But here . . . The roots of the trees web out everywhere, they try to trip her. Supplejack hangs down, and threads in and out like lattice. It is wild and gloomy and terribly green.

Maud looked through the window, and saw them. Lying on the ballroom floor, so close together that they seemed to have melted into one, was a man and a woman. To begin with, looking was all right — they might have been anyone; it was beautiful. At the window, at first, Maud had merely shivered, awed, as looming ghostlike through the mist of centuries, the form of the great Lancelot moved. At first, the window revealed high romance; then Maud saw properly, Tempe made her. She recognized them and what they did, and knew herself deceived.

And so she runs for Papa and Home; yet runs towards poisonous berries and treacherous roots and the rata vine that twines and encircles, and smothers the tops of trees with a cloud of crimson blossom — till, weakened by lack of sunlight, the tree eventually dies.

And, at The Peach Groves, to begin with, it is just another day. Last night there was a ball, and today will mean tidying up. To begin with, Maud's absence doesn't mean much. People drift down from their rooms, yawning; minds still giddy from last night's dance tunes and: "Oh, my head aches something terrible — sherry negus is potent tipple" and: "Did you notice how she danced with him twice; how he took her behind the scrapwork screen?" Maud is missing, but no one seems much concerned. Porridge is spooned-up in a dream, till: "No Maud . . . not upstairs, you say . . . curious, I wonder where?" People frown a little, then, as they think of her from their different viewpoints; but, slowly, most of their minds drift off to last night again. They sit together at breakfast, but they are all irrevocably separate.

Blanche Dean has a preoccupied look and shadows under her eyes; Mrs Maufe appears strangely distraught but, really, it signifies little, for after all that dancing she was taken with a fit of drawing — Wifey is always peculiar after an artistic turn; Ida hasn't said a word since she sat down — a queer creature, Ida . . . too knowing, sly, not like a child at all; Tempe is quiet, too, but not to worry, for she smiles constantly and is especially attentive to Blanche. Queenie and Ethel are happy enough. Ethel severed ties with Grace Darling to write the poem of her life; Queenie met this man with shiny toe-caps . . . he was so nice, he stared and stared — but bashfully, in the best of taste (he stared at his toes) . . . he would not take a snub nor the cold shoulder, he has promised to call. Octavius, however, despite an agitated thumb seems sunk in morbid melancholy, while his Papa looks decidedly worried.

But she only went for a walk to the end of the drive. She is only fairy-sighting at the bottom of the garden. Or fallen asleep under the hawthorn-tree.

But Ida has started to cry. Silly child. She is crying and crying and Tempe has got to her first. She is holding her tight, she is whispering comforting words. ("Don't tell," whispers Tempe. "If you tell what you saw I will kill her — she won't be Mama then, but only a dead dolly all bruised and blue. Don't you dare tell.")

The grown-ups crowd about with handkerchiefs, and Ida sobs out the reason for her tears. Maud has run away. This morning, for no reason at all, she ran out of bed and down the stairs, ran out of the house and into the forest . . .

Ida is hysterical now, and doesn't make sense, but it is Mrs Maufe who screams and falls on the floor. Things start happening. Ethel applies smelling-salts and Tempe slaps Ida's face. It is interesting to feel your cheek tingle like that. Ida stops crying to savour the hurt, and watches Wifey be dragged off to bed and Mr Maufe set about organizing a search-party, which means that a bell rings and men in moleskin pants jump out of Mr Maufe's paddocks. Their work-boots bruise the lawn and strike at the verandah's tessellated stars. "Poor kiddy," they say when they hear about Maud, and Mama dabs her eyes with a lace hanky and they say "Don't worry, Missus, we will find her."

Ida is recovered, now. She sits on at table, alone, and eats up the best pieces of toast, the choicest spoonfuls of marmalade. Maud is missing and Mama says "How could she do it? Why make me suffer so?" Mama is a stranger, now, and Ida even likes her. She did this unmentionable thing with Uncle and, doing it, she offered you a chance to get free. Ida took it and stayed where she was at the window and, watching, knew that Mama could never hurt her again. She wasn't Snow Queen perfect at all. She took off her fancy costume, and revealed a body with appetites and a life of its own.

And it is interesting, but awful. Maud is lost and will never come back. Ida sits safe at The Peach Groves and wipes away toast crumbs, while Mama, who caused it all, says "Why did she do it?" Mama walks about, cries, but even as she says Maud's name, you know she doesn't really care. Interesting. Uncle is Mama's true love, not Maud. And the *cooees* fan out and the men in moleskin pants tramp further into the forest, and now Tempe has put on her boots and says she will search, too.

Maud has fallen. She hides in a jungle of grass choked with bidi-bidi and fiddle-heads and green-hooded orchids. Her skin is pricked and torn, her nightie is smeared with blood; she is stuck all over with burrs, stung by a mad host of whirring whining insects, and so afraid. For she will never ever get back. Mama did this terrible thing and all the world is changed. Never ever, for ever ... The grass is kind: it is a green curtain that shuts out the sky, a

PART FOUR

Epsom; Melbourne

wave that swells and sweeps Maud into dreamless sleep. Nearer and nearer come the cries of her pursuers, but she doesn't hear them.

It was Tempe who found her. Tempe who parted the grass and smiled Maud's sleeping face awake. Sunburned arms came down then, and Maud was gathered up. Oc was there, then; his moon face hung over her, he blocked out Tempe's pointed teeth. Saved, and old Mr Maufe has broken down; his old man's shoulders are racked with sobs — he didn't want little white girl to die (not yet, not yet). They carry her back through the forest, and someone runs on ahead. As they come up through the garden the bell is ringing to tell that she is found.

. . . down-river there are peach-trees. They provided Mr Maufe with a name for his estate; he took Mrs Dean and the little girls to see them, that day they had a picnic. They reached into the leafy trees to pick peaches, they couldn't stop eating — juice ran down their arms, peach flesh stuck between their teeth. Even then a few peaches were falling. They lay pink and gold in the grass, but they still looked good enough to eat, though: What a shame, said Mama when she saw the bruise. But now the trees bear only leaves, the fruit has all fallen off. Peaches fell through the day, through the night, with a steady soft thud. Now there is a horrid smell — rank and ripe — there is a stink of over-sweet jam. Firm peach flesh has turned flabby and wrinkled. No pink and gold sun-up tones now, but only a sad dun-brown. Bees stumble, fumble. The rotting peaches are threaded with ants and flies; veiled by a cloud of whirl-wing midges.

1

Cissie had this brooch. It was gold, fashioned like a
cupid's bow and arrows. Harry had given it to her
once — he loved her then: they weren't married. In
those days, when Cissie was still Miss Wimperis,
Harry had written her letters. "Beloved, dear, dear,
my dear" one of the best had begun; though they
were mostly addressed to "Dear little Sunbeam" or
"Ideal Dream". Cissie used to walk round with
Harry's letters down the front of her dress. The
paper felt scratchy against her skin; it seemed a
wicked thing to do. It was thrilling to know that
Harry's words were there, folded against her skinny
chest. They told how Cissie had changed him so
much; had overturned his every thought and feeling. She was "Sunbeam" because she was a ray of
light in Harry's darkness — a quite exceptional little
being.

The time he said that the emotion with which she
had at first inspired him had deepened into the
passionate adoration of a lifetime, Cissie thought

she would faint. Life got wonderfully physical. She used to lie in bed and long for the touch of Harry's hands. Oh, to look into his eyes; ah, to be kissed. Cissie longed for Harry so much, that she took a girdle and bound it tightly — so tight she could hardly breathe — round her waist and shut her eyes and dreamed it was Harry's arms about her. It gave her almost the feeling; she started lacing her corsets tight.

But then they were married, then a baby never came; Harry didn't love her. He was Major Jones, though she never knew what war he'd been in; he had a strong brown body and a curly beard, but he wasn't like a man at all.

The only baby Cissie had was her aloe. It was a spiteful child, prickly, unrespondent to Cissie's soothing fingers. It gave her some terrible nips, but Cissie kept on loving it. Lately, she'd started doing a curious thing. What she did was to empty her chamber-pot each morning round the aloe's base. Urine was a wonderful tonic for plants, Rachel Hunt had confided.

Mrs Hunt had been Miss Isaacs. In Wellington, there'd been the Nathans; in Auckland, it was an Isaacs who was all right to snub. But Rachel was Cissie's best friend — really, she was Cissie's only friend. It wasn't that Cissie liked her so much — in fact, there was something about Rachel that made her feel stange; that frightened her, almost.

Rachel was all the things that Cissie wasn't. She was small and rosy and sparkling; her hair was jet-black. She wasn't pretty, though; she had a monkey-ish face . . . but this lovely round bosom — a pigeon bosom, so soft. Oh, one day they talked and talked;

that day the gem scones were delicious, the tea was good, too, and Rachel's eyes were kind. Without meaning to, Cissie told about how Harry was happiest with horses — she was disloyal, she couldn't help it. *Yes*, said Rachel Hunt's eyes, *tell me*, and Cissie was just going to — going to tell how awful it was and how she'd go mad if he didn't touch her, when Rachel Hunt moved closer. "Hush, hush," Rachel said, "Oh, dear love." She had her arms round Cissie, she had forced Cissie's head down on her bosom. It was soft; it was nice resting there. "Hush," said Rachel and her small hand was stroking, patting... she used lily-of-the-valley powder... but she had hairs above her lip.

Harry had this sister and he loved *her* all right, he wrote her a letter every week. For years, Cissie had felt jealous of Blanche. And then Cissie took sick; then Blanche Dean came to visit. But Harry didn't seem pleased to see her — he didn't pay her much attention.

The worst thing about Blanche was that she had children. Ida and Maud were a constant reminder of Cissie's barrenness; the relief was wonderful when they went to stay with the Maufes. Cissie wished that they might never return. She felt a different person, too, with Tempe's smirking face nowhere near.

For a while Cissie had hope. They still lived like brother and sister, but their relationship relaxed to a fond one. A lot of Harry's ill-temper was Tempe's fault — she rubbed him up the wrong way as much as she did Cissie. If only they could send her packing; if only they might marry her off. Perhaps that son of the Maufes . . . oh joy, perhaps Tempe would stay at The Peach Groves for ever.

Cissie started blooming. She lingered over pulling up her stockings; she felt like a woman again. Then, what a pity, Harry had to go away. Wapiti was first favourite for the Dunedin Cup and Harry must go south to watch him run. And he went, and Wapiti didn't win, but surely that wasn't reason enough to cause the change. For when Harry came back he was a stranger all over again. Even more aloof than before. When Cissie came close, to welcome him home, he shied away as if she was diseased. And he muttered, he tossed in his sleep.

When Harry was in Dunedin something awful must have happened. Cissie was so worried about him, that when the message came that Blanche was returning early, she even felt glad. Despite the presence of Tempe, company might cheer him up.

❦

Maud ran away, but was found. Hands picked her up from the grassy floor of the forest; arms held her and work-boots trod mystery away. A forest didn't signify much — merely trees, ferns, moss; some birds, many insects.

But not long ago it had been the most terrible place in the world. There was supplejack and kidney fern and the orchid that ate men alive. There were secret drippings and old gods out to get you.

The search-party found her. They were big men, brown and solid. Their voices sounded harsh; they breathed through hairy nostrils. They were common men, there wasn't a gentleman amongst them, but the stink of their sweat made you think of a garden.

Maud gave herself up to being rescued. Her body ached all over, yet, swooning with pleasure, she rode homeward in a stranger's arms.

Yet it wasn't Home when she got there. It was still New Zealand; it was only The Peach Groves. It was ridiculous to have run so far, only to find yourself, at journey's end, come back to where you'd started; to be confronted by what you'd run from.

Mama stood on the verandah. She flew forward, tiptoe, when she saw them coming. Ida ran, too. Maud was still alive and imagine — you could see up her nightie, and she was pressed against the workman's flannel shirt. Usually Ida's big sister was particular where she put her nose; but this looked like a new Maud. Her hair was tangled with thorns and small twigs, there was blood on her legs.

It was the blood that worried Mama most. "Oh dear God," she cried, "not this, too," and she sent the maid to fetch a blanket and then there weren't any men allowed in the room. Maud lay in her blanket on the bed, and Mama was tutting and dipping the flannel into the bowl of steaming water. And there was iodine and Maud had come awake — she was wincing, giving little screams. When she saw the blood she started to cry. "Hush, dear heart," soothed Mama, "it is part of being a woman."

Maud had begun to be grown-up and it wasn't suitable that she should sleep in the same bed as Ida. She went into Mama's room, and, behind the door, Mama must be asking questions: Why did you run away? Why don't you answer?

Mama and Maud weren't the same any more.

Mama looked half dreamy, half worried. She'd begin smoothing her body with her hands, then snatch them away. Then she'd become a proper mama, stiff and bossy. Had they kissed Miss Queenie Maufe goodbye? she asked. What about Miss Ethel? For Maud had run away and started her monthlies and: "Really," said Mama, "it is time we were off." Mr Maufe reminded her that they hadn't seen the hot springs, but Mama stayed firm. Ida felt sorry — Oc was almost like a brother, she would miss Zillah awfully — but Maud didn't seem to care. She didn't look back as the waggonette started off, even though Oc had tears on his cheeks and Mrs Maufe had removed her eye-shade so she might follow their departure better. She even sat stiff as a statue when Mr Maufe pinched her cheek and said that it wasn't really goodbye.

Maud was a different person. She hardly spoke; she had a sullen look, sulky. But worst of all was the way she was always going off in corners with Tempe. They giggled together; they linked arms. In the coach and then the train to Auckland they sat with their elbows touching. Ida shivered, for it seemed that Maud had turned into Tempe's creature. Mama smiled fondly, blindly, pleased that her pets were chums.

2

Blanche had sensitive skin: the mosquitoes at The Peach Groves were fearful. Maybe it was the fault of the bites, for, as soon as she got back to Epsom, she was feverish and ill. Cissie recommended Dr Cobbett who provided a cooling medicine and lotion — but Blanche still itched unmercifully.

It was hot at Epsom. The windows of the drawing-room were always closed, and oh! it was stuffy, and the dining-room, too.

The heat was depressing and relaxing and, sitting in her bedroom, trying to write to George, Blanche longed to be somewhere cool. She felt as bad as she did when there was a heat-wave in Adelaide. Oh to be in green England, a little land, where the sun was discreet, for, sometimes in summer, Adelaide wasn't civilized at all. It was Queen City of the South, but the dust was all about you; the tram tickets flew in the air and the crow's-feet tightened round your eyes. Your complexion would be ruined and the Post Office tower didn't mean a thing, nor your dress of Indian pongee.

Suddenly at Epsom, writing to George, Blanche felt that she couldn't breathe. Then she started having the headache and then she couldn't sit up and she called out to Cissie who came running and put her to bed. Fortunately, Blanche had brought some of the medicine from home with her that she always took and, as usual, it set her right; but for a while she thought there was every chance of not getting over it. Of course, she didn't let the children know how very ill she felt, but Ida was frightened because she couldn't eat anything and looked so weak. Cissie wanted to send for Dr Cobbett but Blanche didn't trust him, though she had every faith in dear old Dr Campbell at Glenelg and only wished he was there. She was glad she'd brought his prescriptions and medicine. She fancied the medicine she had from Dr Cobbett upset her; it was for the great irritation of the mosquito bites. And she was also very tired after the journey, and she may have caught a chill. Anyhow, for a while she never felt worse.

She had lain there with this severe pain in her head, this burning feeling all over her body. And then her body felt cold, she shivered; and now her body was twisting in various directions — her limbs were variously agitated, her hands were clenched. And then she couldn't help it, but part of her seemed to float above the bed and watch the poor sufferer who lay there — who sobbed and cried, laughed and screamed, uttered incoherent expressions and appeared altogether delirious. Then she was unconscious, she recollected nothing. When the fit was over, her headache wasn't so bad, though her body felt sore.

Thank God, though, that Cissie had been out in

the garden when she'd had the turn; that the house had been empty of all but the servants; that no one who counted had heard. Blanche had felt terrible. It was a punishment. But also one of God's unexpected gifts. For the sickness gave her a breathing space. The convulsions and hysterics over, she felt weak but wonderfully calm.

She had time to think. She lay back on soft pillows and felt like a nun. She didn't have to hide; to worry that she might pass him in the passage; to keep her head lowered at table.

How could she have let him do it? How could he have dared to take her like that?

And yet she had wanted it to happen so much. From the first time she saw him — the tall stranger: Hamlet, bearded, in black velvet. She'd seen him watching her. The mask was sinister, yet attractive.

And then he'd claimed her for the polka, then they romped through a mad schottische, and she knew him, she was sure . . . but who? They danced and danced and, after supper, sat together under the flowering jasmine. He didn't speak, he only held her hand. She left him to see to the little girls, and when she returned he was still there. But he was different now; he leant against her heavily and she held him, comforted him. Then he sighed as if he'd made a decision and led her back to the house. The fancy ball was over, now; one by one the revellers had departed.

The ballroom was theirs, alone, and they circled once or twice in a decorous waltz. But then he pulled her to him; then she pushed back the mask, and saw him as Harry. He said they did wrong, but she only laughed. She told him she had known it was he all along (had she? — unknowing, did she tell the truth?).

That morning in the ballroom they'd made all sorts of promises. Their love would last for ever. They must never live separate again. She would give up George and the girls; he'd sacrifice his horses and Cissie. They'd sail back to England — live anywhere. She'd be Bets again; he'd leave off the "Major" and go back to the patent medicines.

Living in a little house would be romantic. She'd simplify her life: cook greens for his supper and ruin her hands scrubbing and come down with the flu every winter. (Winter in England could be awful. Blanche had delicate ears, and sometimes in winter in England, the cold was so bad that it seemed that knitting-needles were stuck in your ear-drums.)

Harry started back for Epsom and the task of telling Cissie that he'd be off. Blanche curled up between best linen sheets and wondered how she'd bear sleeping between cheap ones . . . or would they be so poor that they wouldn't have sheets at all? And in not too many years she'd be forty — would he still love her then?

All that day Blanche worried over what she should do — go off with the one; stay put with the other? One instant her body cried out for Harry; the next, her mind plumped for George.

That day was one of the worst. Maud was inconsiderate enough to choose it to run away on and Blanche, as well as worrying, must remember to cry dutifully and to say "Please God" every so often, as befitted a grieving mama. but all the time she thought of Harry, of George. Which one should it be, which life should she choose?

Well, she still hadn't decided when the train reached Auckland. Getting off, she held her stomach in carefully, for Harry would be watching, waiting on the platform . . . But he wasn't — only the coachman was there.

Blanche knew that something was wrong, and wondered if it might be Cissie. She dreaded seeing her; dreaded the fuss that Harry's news would have caused: Cissie might do anything . . . But she didn't. She welcomed them with a smile, she was exactly the same. Blanche scratched her mosquito bites absently and felt disappointed that she took it so calmly. But Harry wasn't in the house — Cissie said something about a sick horse and Blanche knew something was up. She burned with mortification; she had a suspicion that Harry's had been the feelings that cooled first.

Even though she felt ill and feverish, she was ready for him when he appeared to eat dinner. She matched his nerve with an eye just as cool. Oh yes, she said without even a blush, they'd spent a most agreeable visit with the Maufes. "There was a fancy ball, you know," she said daringly. "What a pity you and Cissie couldn't make it."

Harry smiled as if he hated her; he asked when they were leaving for Glenelg. Blanche could have killed him. The time for their departure couldn't come soon enough, she was going to say, when Cissie chipped in before her.

Cissie wanted them to stay. "Just a little longer," she pleaded, wheedling. And then it came out that the minx had sent an invite to Mr Maufe. Cissie was only trying to be helpful . . . he was an old man with not much to live for, and so interested in Master

187

Bob's music... And the great violinist, Remenyi, was coming to Auckland and Mr Maufe, being well-connected, knew him and would surely drop a word... "Oh please," begged Cissie, "just till the end of next week."

Harry sat there, terribly silent, but Cissie didn't seem to notice. She was babbling happily about how young Mr Maufe would be coming, too. Cissie had never met the lad, but if he resembled his papa, he'd be charming. It would be nice for Tempe to have a young gentleman close at hand, said Cissie, coyly.

Tempe was laughing into her hanky, and Maud looked bored and Ida bewildered, and Harry frowned worse. Blanche felt hotter and itchier and couldn't sit there another minute. She excused herself and went off to write to George, to tell him they'd be leaving immediately. Which was when she had the attack.

Bed was the best place to be. Blanche took her medicine and suffered Cissie's fussing and for the first time in ages felt free. She'd done the wicked thing again with Harry and God had punished her by nearly making her die. It was a close thing, but He had relented: Blanche had recovered and decided that never more would her body rule her. It was a sin, what they'd done in the ballroom; being beautiful didn't excuse it. Beauty — and Blanche's lip curled fetchingly — wouldn't mean anything now. She'd be a changed person inside; though on the surface, of course, she'd have to go on pretending. She was George's wife, it was her duty. When she and the chicks got back to Glenelg, Blanche rather thought a dinner party, very select . . . for which she'd need a new gown. Cherry silk, Blanche rather thought.

They'd go home; life would continue. But for now they'd stay those few extra days. It would be good to see Mr Maufe again — and so soon after leaving him.

Blanche lay back on her pillows and smiled. She'd rest in bed a little longer, for she needed time to recover her strength, to make herself strong enough to face Harry. It had been a sin, but they'd wipe it quite out. "You will always mean more to me than anyone," she'd say kindly, "but we must never meet again."

God forgave her; Harry would, too. What they'd done signified little. No one had seen them, no one would know. It was but a small sin: no one was hurt.

"My dear old darling," Mama's letter began and, who'd believe it? — she wrote to Papa. Ida kept reading while Mama slept on: Papa's wee note had kindled a glow of pleasure — so he really missed her a jot! Mama missed him so much, that she didn't intend to leave him ever again . . . Ida's eye scanned the next lines fast, for they merely concerned Mama's health: "too uncertain to be away from you for long . . . no place like home . . . This attack and feeling so weak after it, has determined me to take the greatest care of your precious property, my lord!" They expected to leave Epsom about next Friday, on either the *Rotomahana* (Cap. Carey) or the *Tarawera* (Cap. Sinclair) — it couldn't be earlier, because Mr Maufe and Octavius were coming especially to bid a last goodbye. Which led on to their stay at The Peach Groves, where: "Ida won much love and attention, but Maud was first favourite." Another boring part followed. Ida skipped several *my very own darlings* till her eye caught further mention of the Maufes. First she read quickly, for Mama only told of how much interest Mr M. took in Maud's music; then Octavius's name appeared and Ida read slowly, savouring each word, for: "Octavius, according to Cissie, will serve as an admirable suitor for Tempe" — though Mama thought the match unlikely.

Then Mama's eyelashes fluttered, and Ida edged back from "Consider yourself kissed" and "I'm like Juliet in one thing: 'I could say good night until tomorrow' when once I begin writing to you" and tried to look innocent, unknowing.

But Mama frowned when she saw her in the room; she eyed her letter to Papa suspiciously. "You are always lurking, child," she accused, and her voice didn't sound sickly as it drove Ida into the garden.

Which was a pleasant place to be, as long as you kept clear of Auntie's aloe. During their time away it seemed to have grown larger; there was a funny smell all round it, and a lot of baby aloes at its base — they looked like rabbits' ears; a scalloping line of baby thorns sprouted already at the edge of each leaf. Auntie's hydrangeas were brown and screwed, now, and there weren't many roses left, but the geraniums still bloomed, the fuchsia bells hadn't yet dropped. The pine-trees were full of velvet shadows; Mount Eden and Mount St John stood in their places; you'd never connect the tennis-lawn's silken expanse with mere grass.

Once past the lawn, you approached the coach-man's cottage. The coachman's wife had recently presented him with a son, and so Aunt Cissie had another thing to fuss about besides her aloe and Mama's health. She'd been immensely interested in Baby's arrival and was constantly running down to the cottage. She hurried past Ida now, with a laden basket on her arm and a fierce expression — yet a wistful one, too — on her face. "Poor little woman," Mama had said of Auntie, once, to Tempe, "she would give anything to have a child of her own." Mama had never realized before how much child-less women missed — especially those who had nice homes and gardens. "Of course," she added tartly, "Cissie is sure that any child of hers would be perfect." (Tempe knew the old adage about bachelors' wives and old maids' children).

Ida sighed, for everything was muddled. Since their return to Epsom, Auntie spoke to Tempe in honeyed tones and was anxious to provide her with a bridegroom-elect. Yet Auntie disliked Tempe intensely, just as Mama entertained similar feelings for Auntie... and Mama, who had loved Uncle Harry, now pledged herself to Papa and didn't face up to Maud's stony demeanour or the vengeful look in Tempe's eyes. And Tempe? — what power did she have that bound Maud so close to her; why, even now, was she leading her into the pine-wood that bordered Auntie's garden?

How could Maud allow Tempe to link her arm like that; how step so easily from the bright garden shimmering with light, to enter the forest's dimness? Auntie's aloe might smell of pee and reach after you with thorny leaves, but the garden was mostly a safe place, even though the ghost of the fox buried under Auntie's Provence rose came out of the earth at night, and dragged its bushy tail against the house and . . . But not true — it was only a story, and Ida made it up; that night-time sound had been just the wind in Auntie's kowhai-tree, and that tree was pretty, its flowers made a golden rain . . . Despite Auntie's garden being mostly neat and the bushes kept clipped with secateurs, it was a nice place to be. There were coin-spot butterflies and bees in the sunflowers and Maud was a silly to leave it, to forget that the last time she went into a forest she nearly stayed there for ever. How could she walk under the pine-trees so heedless, with her pale hand caged by Tempe's tanned one?

Maud looked so innocent with her hair hanging down her back and her baby-blue sash round her waist — yet Tempe linked her close, her hip nudged her hard. The pine-trees rose shaggy above them and no birds sang; the silence was full of whispers. Pine-cones and dried needles littered the earth. If you pretended a little, the cones looked like the skulls of dead babies. Ida shivered deliciously, and kept up her rôle of faithful shadow. She flitted noiselessly behind them as they took the familiar path to the pool.

This time, though, Tempe didn't carry the dress she wore when she floated there and sang her crazy song at the sky. Like Aunt Cissie, she carried a basket. Perhaps Tempe and Maud were off on a picnic?

Yet Maud didn't appear to anticipate a treat. She

moved listlessly, as if in a dream; her eyes gazed straight ahead. Then, just before the jungly part of the walk began, she sank down beside Tempe on the trunk of a fallen tree. Tempe's hand reached into her basket and emerged with something that shone — Ida peeped out and saw it was a little bottle, a phial. Maud drank from it eagerly; drank till the phial was drained, then licked her lips contentedly. When she rose she rubbed her eyes as if she felt sleepy and, though she kept walking, she dragged her feet. Now Maud was more of a sleep-walker than ever, and Tempe seized her chance to edge closer. She had her arm round Maud's waist as she guided her through a dank green world. Then they were going downhill and into the ruined garden where plumbago foamed in the hibiscus bush and Venus was garlanded with pumpkin flowers; where ivy tangled everywhere and fluttered like a curtain before a cave lined with shells.

Just before they came to the cave they halted again. Nearby was the statue of Cupid and it was a pity that his marble eyes were masked with creeper, because next came a regular poppy-show. Tempe was unbuttoning Maud's dress and pulling down her petticoat; then she examined Maud's chest as if she played Doctor. She squeezed the small breasts, she tested their nipples with her tongue — and Maud let her; she stood unmoved, as passive as Cupid on his pedestal — even when Tempe felt under her skirt. It should have been shameful but it wasn't; it was all done so coldly that it didn't seem unnatural at all. Tempe fastened Maud's buttons briskly and plucked a stray leaf from her hair. When everything was to rights again, they proceeded towards the cave.

Outside its tangled drape of ivy a figure waited. It was the camel-boy from the circus and he waved when he saw them approach. He'd left off the Fairy Prince outfit; now the leopard skin served as a loincloth and he wore beads round his neck. Tempe seemed to approve of his appearance. She ran into his arms and: "Oh Ed," she cried, and they kissed as if they'd been parted for years, till suddenly Tempe pulled away.

She didn't call him Ed, now, but Tane. It was a queer-sounding name, but the camel-boy answered to it. He rumpled Tempe's hair fondly as if he was used to her quirks; he smiled good-naturedly as he shook hands with Maud. It was striking to see the pair of them together: Maud, who even after a tramp through the forest, and the attentions of Tempe's clinical fingers, was still pale and neat as a pin; the camel-boy, berry-brown, with his black hair hanging round his shoulders in curly tendrils.

Then he shouted out that he was starving, and he seized Tempe's basket and his teeth bit into steak and kidney pie. There were all sorts of things in the basket — some cheese and a pot of jam and a loaf of bread. The camel-boy didn't bother with a knife, but tore at the loaf with his fingers.

Maud sat demurely beside him — he was common, but she didn't flinch. The camel-boy didn't seem to mind her blank stare, though; he said that it was good to have company at last. It wasn't much chop keeping low in a cave.

Maud sat there, as if she was under the stupefying influence of a drug. She was only a clockwork dolly, and Tempe could whisper in her ear and dolly would do her bidding. It looked like that, anyway, to Ida watching. For Tempe said something that made Maud come alive. Ed stopped picking his nose, for Maud was smiling at him now. She looked as if her mind was occupied with lascivious thoughts; she wriggled, and started fiddling with her buttons — then she was sliding her dress off her shoulders; till she was right out of it, till she lay at Ed's feet, a lovely half thing — not child, not woman — terribly exposed. Maud's body squirmed on the grass as if it burned and prickled and tingled — it was pink and terribly alive.

Maud seemed wild with desire; it was as if she had a disease (maybe an oozing tumour). Yet, though she twitched below waist, the sickness seemed mainly in her brain. It was as if a disgusting enemy had got into Maud's head and her body tried to shake it off. Perhaps she should stick to a fruitarian diet, for last night's dinner had been mutton curry, and fiery seasonings inflamed the blood. Poor Maud — she ought to wear a wet genital pad to cool herself down, or try a piece of ice in the rectum. The male society with which she associated should be intellectual and, above everything else, pure-minded.

Eddie Thrush wasn't a gent, but he seemed to fit the bill here. For he looked at Maud with horror, as if she committed chastity's grossest breach. And then Ed Thrush lunged out for dear old Mum: he kicked at Maud with his foot; he hit Tempe on the face, he spat at her. "Bitch," he called her, and: "Dirty cow." His hand left a red mark on Tempe's cheek, and she rubbed it bemusedly as he strode past Cupid and Venus. Maud lay on the grass like a dead thing, now. She whimpered as Tempe jerked her into her clothes.

Ida left the cover of the bushes she'd sheltered behind all that time; she stopped caring that they shouldn't see her, she started running back. Now she knew how Maud had felt when she tried to run from Mama. It had been awful, what she'd seen — she'd never forget. Nothing could ever be worse ... not even the dead bird that lay in Ida's path. Its body was broken, its breast was eaten with ants. Not worse, but the bird made Ida cry. Oh God, she cried, oh Queechy. Was home still there, would they ever be themselves again?

3

Tempe often had a companion, now, who accompanied her through each day. Because of Mother being inside her, Tempe could walk about big — she was a giant treading the days out, kicking them into order with stylish six-league boots. She felt important, terribly powerful from the moment she woke up. Another day, and the sun came in at the window, the sky flamed with light. Tempe was awake, and the new day could begin. Mount Eden poked up to say Good morning, and Mother and Tempe would show them — they'd climb the mountain together; they'd throw their voices at the crater and: *Beautiful, beautiful* the crater answered back. Oh, and they *were* comely — Mother and Tempe. And proper ladies, too, and no one at Government House would dare to snub. They walked into the ballroom on a small wind of appreciative gasps. Mother was Linda, with chalk-white skin and the Maori gone out of her nose. There was no crinkle in her hair when Father asked her to dance.

Sometimes, though, she was another — the day started differently, then. Those days, Mother made Tempe wake up before the sun. The day was still sleeping, but Mother banged at Tempe's head; she wailed in her ear; she wouldn't be ignored. "Remember, remember," cried Mother, but Tempe couldn't — Mother was a grey ghost and Tempe couldn't recall her name. "Not Linda — no never," Mother cried on days like that. She banged at Tempe's head all day; the headache was awful, and Tempe hated Cissie worse. Somehow it was Cissie's fault that Tempe had lost Mother's name. "Shall I make her die, then?" Tempe asked Mother, and the headache eased, while she considered. "Not Cissie, not this time," Mother decided at last. "Not her, but that other one — Harry's sister, she should suffer now." What Blanche Dean did with Harry deserved a bad scare. It was all right to give Blanche poisonous berries. Serve her right that she felt the pain — the hot and the cold, the knife in the heart — just like Tempe had when she saw Harry love her.

When they'd wandered together in the forest, Tempe held Mother's hand. Tempe was allowed to be a child, magic was everywhere. The bushes were full of berries — pink ones, red; the sun came through the leaves in spangles. Tempe was small and so happy; Mother was lovely but strong. She put out her hand and seed-pods rattled, bright berries fell into her basket. Yet danger was all about you. A white bird signified misfortune; a lizard was an omen of death. A misty day could be tricky, too, for on misty days you heard fairy flutes in the distance and pretty girls wandered away. Some fairies were but as big as your thumb, others had China-

man's fingernails. Sea fairies came ashore only at
night: sea fairies died in the sun.

Once Tempe knew Mother's stories by heart.
How the woman got into the moon. How Sky
Father and Earth Mother were separated and his
tears fell as rain, the mists were a token of her love.
How Tane brought the sacred baskets of knowledge
to earth . . . Tane was the only god whose name
Mother let Tempe recall. Tane was the great forest
god; the father of all trees and black birds. Tane
allowed babies to be born; he had twenty children
of his own in each of the Twelve Heavens, and after
he formed woman of the earth he gave her a baby,
too, and this time Tane's child was the goddess of
death.

Tempe understood it all once, but now most of
the words were forgotten; those that she remembered didn't always seem true. Sometimes she
believed in Tane, other times not. Sometimes it was
true that Mother had sent him to walk on the earth.

It was a funny world that Tempe lived in, now. It
was New Zealand where titoki and karaka grew,
but Cissie's garden was pure England. Tane and
Mother were muddled in Tempe's head with
Alfred, Lord T. and the Lady of Shalott.

Mother told her stories again when Tempe floated like Tennyson's Lady in the pool: Tempe always
felt the better for a dip. But Mother could stop playing fair. Sometimes Tempe woke up lonely, and the
sun was a blind glassy eye; the wind was a wolf
down the chimney; the lightning was God's lasso.
Sometimes Tempe shivered under the bedclothes
and wanted to disappear. She hated living at Epsom
with apostle spoons and Cissie. She'd tried to make

it Mother's room she lived in, but often Mother was nowhere near.

Tempe was two people, really. There was the one who lived for Linda; there was the other who lived as a body. The two parts of Tempe were quite separate; what one did the other didn't know. One Tempe had a friend called Eddie Thrush, the other was acquainted with Tane.

Tane wasn't any help when Harry let Tempe down; Ed Thrush wasn't, either. The Tempe who knew Tane didn't know Harry; the Tempe who knew Ed had been sure he'd help with revenge. For there was this little prig, Maud. She looked just like her mama; she was Blanche Dean's image. The best way to hurt Blanche most of all, would be to turn Maud as bad as herself. To treat her like a devil's dolly — drag her down in the mud; pluck out her bright child's heart and replace it with something only fit for the butcher's window. Priggish Maud would end up as a shambles; Tempe knew of potions that would bring on her ruin fast. Ed had been meant to help, for Tempe would sacrifice anything to wound Blanche — even the camel-boy.

But Ed wouldn't. Because of Maud Dean, he hit Tempe's face; he ran from Tempe's life for ever. Maud scared him away and Tempe would never forgive her. Maud would pay even worse.

Tempe had no one, now, for her body. It cried out at night and Mother's skeleton fingers were no good as fleshly comforters. It would be unbearable tomorrow at breakfast. Harry would sit across the table from Tempe, and Harry had made himself a stranger. She would see him and know what she'd lost. And there'd be no camel-boy to make up for it, for Tempe had lost him, too. She would have no one at all. Oh, bed was a lonely place, a body was a sad thing to have.

But Tempe had her mind, she had Mother. It was still summer and the sun shone every day. Mount Eden was Tempe's own mountain and she could still be a giant — still pronounce, if she chose to, that Blanche Dean should die. It was even a good thing that Tempe had the headaches, for a headache was merely Mother knocking; a bad head meant that Mother cared. And Tempe was still privileged to know Tane. He was a great god, but sometimes he let her see him. Perhaps Tane — life-giver, fertilizer, sustainer — might even give Tempe a baby . . . A child would mean she'd never be lonely again.

❧

There were dead birds all over the forest, it wasn't a nice place to be. Overnight, dead birds fell like rain. Out of the sky and the trees' leafy branches. Birds fell, and blood streamed from the birds' dead breasts and feathers fell, too, like snow. Perhaps a giant cat jumped into the sky and killed all the birds — bit off their heads, ripped off their wings. Poor birds. The forest at the bottom of Auntie's garden wasn't a safe place for fantail or tui.

Well, several birds were dead in the forest. The next one Ida saw was the pigeon. She nearly walked on its white breast. Poor bird, its neck was all screwed. Ida covered it with leaves, she felt virtuous. But when she first saw it she'd felt something else — a panicky jerk, a jolt deep inside her; before Ida's eyes really knew what they saw, her body signalled

Death. Her body knew with animal instinct. *Dead, dead* it told her, and her foot jumped back just in time.

Someone was killing the birds. And didn't they know that to tamper with a pigeon was dangerous? — for he who was sprinkled with pigeon's blood would never die natural. A pigeon sitting in a tree was regarded as a sign of death. It was a bad omen, too, if an invalid asked for pigeons to eat. And with pigeons' feathers in a bed, people died hard.

But the next dead bird that Ida found was the fluffy little owl. It only came out at night (someone was killing at night); "More pork, more pork" it cried and it liked to catch a rat for its supper. But someone caught the night owl first. There was no warmth in its fluffy feathers, now.

You came in from the forest to Auntie's drawing-room. The cottage on the painted pebble had roses round the door, and though Mr Maufe was coming, Octavius would come too. But even in Aunt Cissie's drawing-room Ida remembered the birds. Why had they died, who had done it? You couldn't use God as an excuse, for the owl had a noose round its neck.

It must have hurt the birds to die, but the sunlight in Auntie's drawing-room was placid, the afternoon-tea cloth had a dainty crochet border to mask its stiff damask edge. And the coachman's baby was a monster, little darling. He slept all day and roared all night; he was born with a rupture in his private parts, but Doctor tied them up tight with his napkin and Baby was on the mend, Auntie was pleased to report.

Mama was better also, for Mama had started to complain. Her latest letter to Papa was all about fruit. "I haven't had an apple since we came back to Epsom," Mama wrote to Papa. There were plenty of apples, pears and plums and bananas in the fruit shops in Auckland, but Auntie didn't care to indulge.

Mama loved Papa now; she sent him a goodnight kiss with every letter. Mama wrote to Papa every day, and he wrote back and sent a telegram that said "I love you dearest, also" and two money-orders for ten pounds each and the *Observer*, the *Register* and the *Advertiser*, so that Mama might catch up on Adelaide news. Well, she might have stuck to Lady Kitty's column or Housekeeping Hints, but she didn't. Mama had to turn to News from the Empire and read out about General Gordon's death. Aunt Cissie shook her head and said How dreadful. To think of that grand man being sacrificed for those black wretches.

And Colonel Stewart had died of his wounds, and everyone in Auckland talked of it, and the flags were half-masted on the vessels in the harbour, and seven hundred men from Sydney were off to the Sudan, and Ida's dreams got worse. The birds were in them with their fragile broken bodies, and General Gordon and the black wretches, too.

But Mama was out of bed, now, and soon they'd be going home. The *Tarawera* would take them by way of the southern ports to Melbourne, where Papa would meet them. They'd stay a few days — a family reunited — and then sail back to Adelaide on the *Pekin*.

They would get home. There was no need for Ida to worry and have the nightmares, even though the birds kept dying and Mr Maufe was arriving . . . had arrived: and he stepped down from the waggonette and straight away made for Maud.

In just those few days since they'd left The Peach Groves, Mr Maufe seemed to have aged. He was an ugly old man for sure, now; his mouth kept twitching, he kept licking his lips, there were veins all over his cheeks — a criss-cross web of red and blue lines that made his face look jewelled. He was a sinister Daddy Christmas, with his jewelled face and his sugar crystal moustache. His piggy eyes were more awful than ever as: "Dear little girl," he said mildly, while his hand rested heavy on Maud's shoulder. Mama and Aunt Cissie tittered fondly, but Uncle gave Mr Maufe a long look.

Uncle Harry was another man, too — a different man from all the different men he'd been before. You'd never mistake him for Hamlet or a *Pilgrim's Progress* angel ever again. He looked shrunken, there were lines on his face. He'd started looking like that even before Mama had got up from her sick-bed and written of fruit to Papa and read out about General Gordon and then sat next to Uncle on the sofa while Auntie was petting her aloe. Mama had been like a lady in a play, and Uncle was the poor scoundrel she forgave. "I forgive you, Harry," Mama said graciously, and Uncle might have been a black wretch and Mama the lady missionary, as she told Uncle he was a scamp and an ignoramus and the act was illegal and he could be made to pay the penalties which the law would enforce and the way of transgressors was hard. Ida thought Uncle's mouth twitched, and she wondered for a moment if he'd laugh . . . but it must have been a trick of the light (Ida couldn't see too well, crouched behind the big armchair), for Uncle only nodded his head sadly; he kept his head bowed as he thanked Mama for all her forgiving. Mama looked as if she expected Uncle to say something more; she even looked a little disappointed that he accepted her accusations without demur. But Uncle said hardly anything. Mama broke the silence between them at last, by saying that they'd be leaving Auckland on Friday.

And they'd sail on and on — past Gisborne and Napier and Wellington and Christchurch and Dunedin and Hobart — and sea air would revive Maud wonderfully; Maud would be herself again by the time they got to Melbourne where, on the wharf, Papa would be waiting. Nothing would stop them reaching him. Mr Maufe had come all the way from The Peach Groves to have a try, but Oc had come with him — Ida and Queechy would have an ally in their fight for Maud.

For a confrontation was coming, Ida was sure of it. Something final would have to happen before they were free to leave New Zealand.

Dear Oc (though his habit was so bad that he was more truly Octavius), he was an unlikely helpmate to have. He was terribly nervous. And Aunt Cissie made him worse, for she was always fussing, always shooing him off to be with Tempe. "Show Octavius the garden, my dear," she'd say in her false caring voice. And why didn't Tempe sing her pretty drawing-room song? "None Know How I Love Thee" was the song Auntie meant.

Aunt Cissie seemed as unmindful of Oc's misery as she was of his papa's decidedly negative attitude to Tempe. Once Mr Maufe had been fond of the girl; now her presence seemed to make him uneasy. Tempe appeared to share the old man's feelings: she averted her head when he entered the room. Each was able to disturb the other profoundly; it was as if each knew too much about the other's deepest feelings. Mr Maufe seemed a constant reminder of a humiliation Tempe chose to forget; Tempe appeared able to make Mr Maufe feel weak instead of strong, a sure loser instead of a victor.

Tempe enjoyed Oc's discomfort as he sought to extricate himself from the rôle of reluctant suitor. Perversely, she took pleasure in enacting the part of not so reluctant wooed one. Tempe frightened Oc thoroughly; she smiled sweetly as he flexed his thumb worse.

But when Auntie suggested a *tête-à-tête* tramp to the top of Mount Eden, her attitude changed. Tempe had treated Auntie's scheming as a joke till she said that.

Auntie went into the little room by the pantry where she kept her flower vases, where she arranged her flowers. She'd been out in the garden that morning and she'd picked a big bunch, and she had all the vases ready — they stood ranged in neat marching order, from the glass slipper that did for small flowers like violets, to the urn that tiger-lilies looked best in. Auntie was humming happily and poking cockscombs into twin crystal vases when Tempe came in with her eyes glinting and fierce. Their voices grew louder, until there was a dreadful silence in the house and you knew that the maid had stopped dusting, that Cook had granted the lobster a reprieve from its boiled water bath, to listen. Dust fell and the lobster went on living and

Tempe screamed louder. Ida and Oc crept to the flower-room door and she stood close to Auntie and screamed that it was her mountain, hers and Linda's, and no one else's at all. No one else would ever go there, never ever again — Tempe would see to that. It was Tempe's mountain, it was Linda's. And Linda had been a princess, Linda was pure. Cissie would never speak ill of her again . . .

And now the voice was Aunt Cissie's. The velvety cockscombs were in her hand and Auntie was laughing, then talking. "Linda — your mother — royal blood," she cried. "Pure, you say — Linda? Oh, my God, that's a good one — Linda pure!" And Auntie was bobbing up and down, wheezing, wiping her eyes on her apron and now the cockscombs had fallen to the floor; they drooped sadly, velvety, wine-red and Auntie's shoes were treading them to pieces. "Oh, Linda pure," she cried. "Why, Linda was the worst slut in Wellington. Everyone knew, she was the jest of the town. Everyone who wore trousers had Linda — even Father . . ."

But now Auntie had stopped laughing — she had to, for Tempe had her by the hair. Auntie cried out in pain. Uncoiled, her hair was amazingly thick; it looked alive, so crackly and excited, as it fell round her frightened face. Oc and Ida drew back, afraid, for Tempe might do anything. For a moment she had her hands round Aunt Cissie's throat, but then Auntie managed to push her away and snatch up the scissors she used to snip flower-stalks and she pointed them at Tempe, and all the hate Cissie had felt for all those years — all her rage at *them*, and all her longing for a child — was in her face as she hated Tempe, too — hated and hated her, and raised the hand that held the scissors . . . And she would have stabbed Tempe, only the girl ran out of the room.

Then Auntie lay on the floor amongst the shredded cockscombs; she was shuddering, her face was slippery with tears and the housemaid appeared and Cook, too, and even Mama. Everyone ran to Aunt Cissie, except Oc and Ida, who concentrated on the flower-room window.

The window overlooked the garden, which was where something interesting happened. For Tempe had an axe in her hands — she struck again and again, she hacked like a mad thing. Now Auntie's aloe was nothing to be proud of; now there wasn't much aloe left at all.

4

Cissie's aloe didn't exist and she didn't feel a thing. For years she'd pampered it, petted it, even as its thorns dug deep at her flesh. She'd thought of it as her baby, but she'd felt nothing when she'd seen the pile of mutilated leaves trundle past on the coachman's barrow. The aloe was dead, and Cissie didn't mourn it. All she cared to recall was the surge of rage as her hand swung the scissors in the air. Remember: that silver flash at the tip of your fingers, that weightless feel to your body; your heart leaping, looping and then darkness — then Cissie was down on the floor with the crystal vases smashing about her, and she'd hated so hard, so well, that her body felt fantastically loved — it no longer huddled and hid, all its tensions were worn away: Cissie's body lay loose on the flower-room floor, spread-eagled in lovely abandonment, amongst a mess of broken cockscombs and glass and spilt water. She was wet, she couldn't stop crying, and it felt so good ... really, she should thank Tempe before they sent her away. The girl was crazy, of course — as crazy as Linda before her. Cissie had always hated her, but furtively — with a tight-clenched brand of hate that had festered in a torturous underground way, instead of sparking free. But now Cissie felt good. All her hate had been used up as the scissors cut the air; now she almost pitied Tempe. They would send her away. There were places. But imagine Tempe with a keeper; Tempe living a regular life . . .

And while Cissie failed to imagine it, Tempe sat up in bed. They had dragged her away from the aloe; they had wrenched the axe from her hands. There were so many of them that she couldn't fight free, though she'd given Cook a nasty gash on the arm — Cook's arm bled red and Tempe's head thumped harder, it felt as if her head applauded the deed. But then she was more clever still, then she went limp. They carried her into Mother's room, they took off her clothes. Their clumsy hands touched Tempe's body, they hated her and she let them; she kept her eyes closed and they said she was senseless. It was a good thing, they said, for she was dangerous. Cook held out her arm as evidence, and the housemaid said "She bit me." She'd tried to strangle Cissie, they said, and that bitch Blanche Dean was tapping her head (Tempe peeped out from under her lashes: Blanche Dean meant that Tempe was a loony). But it was Harry who said she must go; Harry who turned traitor first and went to fetch Dr Cobbett. *You fool*, Mother said, *to ever give yourself to him*. No ordinary man was worth Tempe's love. . . only a great god could do her justice: ah yes, Tempe knew she must find Tane. And it was awful

in the room, unbearable, even though her captors
went out, even though it was Mother's room (even
though they'd locked the door). Its tameness
oppressed her. She wanted to smash the knick-
knacks, scrawl obscenities over the rose-and-ribbon
walls; free herself from the terrible tiny clutch of
glove box and hair-tidy. Tempe was tired of being a
lady; of being imprisoned by a fake ladylike room.
The room was a lie and her head hurt bad. But
quick, she must have a leaf — it was another of
Mother's stories. How if you wanted a baby you
must tear a leaf into the shape of a man. A leaf torn
like that made a spell. Tane would come to Tempe,
then. He would fall on her body; she would be safe
in his forest god's embrace. "I will go then," said
Tempe, for she heard Mother's voice tell her to be
off, it was clearly a command. She sat up in bed —
they would never catch her again, never bring her
back. She'd escape them all: Cissie and Harry and
Tennyson and his waterlogged Lady; Blanche Dean
and Ida and Maud and the Maufes. None of them
would pin Tempe down. She'd outwit every one of
them — outwit even part of herself. The Tempe
who had need of a fleshly comforter would be con-
founded, too. And Tempe slipped out of bed; she
pushed up the window and leapt from the sill.

Maud wandered in the garden, wondering who
she was. She wasn't sure if she was anyone; she felt
like a ghost, a very small one. She shivered, even
though the garden was warm and sleepy, and
Auntie's mother-in-law's tongue stood up stiff. It
was a comical plant, that one, but today it couldn't
make Maud laugh. Maud hadn't laughed for a long
time. For ages, now, she hadn't felt a thing. It was

211

like living in a cardboard box. Greyness was all about her, and a soft pappy smell. Recently, though, the softness had been pierced by a shaft of feeling. There was a pain, now — the light had come in, the greyness was shot through with detail. The light hurt Maud's eyes, the colours in the garden were bright. The mother-in-law's tongue was savage; the blades of grass licked her boots. It was strange how these things poked out of the chocolate earth: thin blades of grass, ruffled geraniums, sharp-edged ferns. Then there was a pile of rocks; then, in patches of dirt, grew creeping things — plants like rick-rack braid; then there was a hole . . . the dirt down there was moist and dark like the slice of Christmas cake, and you saw a pattern of roots. The hole made Maud afraid (what plant had grown there?), and she wished that Tempe would give her a drink. For, regularly, Tempe would say "Drink" and, obediently, Maud would do so. She'd feel better then. She wished she felt better now. It seemed a long time since Tempe had given Maud a drink; though, in reality, Maud had drunk from Tempe's bottle yesterday. But, since then, after showing the young gentleman the flower-beds and singing him her song, Tempe had disappeared. Maud couldn't find her anywhere, and she wanted Tempe so much — wanted to drink and feel soft and grey and dead again, so that she needn't bother to wonder; wanted to stare into Tempe's eyes so that she needn't bother to think, but might be told what to do. No Tempe meant that Maud was starting to come awake; starting to think, to remember that she was Maud Dean of Glenelg, who'd come to Epsom with Mama and Ida . . . But it was too painful — coming alive after being dead. And then Maud looked across the lawn; then she saw Tempe climb from the window and run towards the pine-trees. Smiling, Maud began running, too.

Mr Maufe had to follow, of course. All day he'd been Maud's faithful shadow; he'd stuck to her leech-like — she was irresistible. More so than ever, now, for she moved as if in a dream; she played innocent so well that he almost believed in her pose. He'd had to come to Epsom, Cissie's invite had saved his life. When Maud had left him he'd felt bereft. He didn't want any crude substitute; without little white girl his life had no meaning. When she'd left him, nothing would ease his melancholy and the dreary ache in his guts. He had a bottle of Vichy water and a dry biscuit before retiring, but it wasn't productive of a good night's rest, for still he dreamed of her, still he must see her again. He must reach her before anyone else. For anyone else would be the death of the Maud he knew, and time was death, too. For time would get her for certain unless he acted; time had sprung on Maud already. It wasn't as if he'd do wrong. It was a kindness, really, to preserve dear Master Bob as she was now . . .

Octavius saw him go and knew he was meant to save Maud. A person was offered just once a hero's part to play in life. Now Oc's chance to play hero had come and he didn't mean to turn it down. For Maud was in danger, for Oc knew his papa well; knew that Augustus, when roused, was as pug-nacious as a grazing bull who raises his eyes from green herbage to focus on an object in red — and the bull can't help it as he charges; he can't help his excitement, for red is the complementary colour to green and therefore provoking. Oc's papa was just like that bull as he ran after Maud: therefore Octavius ran, too.

And so, of course, does Ida. And, at The Peach Groves, Zillah sits before her sketch-block and the little girl in white starts off on her final outing; for after today, though Zillah doesn't know it, so many things will come to an end — even little white girl, even Zillah's rôle as visionary artist — and a new pattern of living begin. And, as Ida tags Oc (who tags Augustus and Maud and Tempe), Blanche Dean stands on the balcony of Harry's house; and she raises her hand and from it something flies at the sky and then plummets earthward to be lost for ever in Cissie's garden; and it is the kauri-gum heart that Blanche has thrown away — Harry gave it to her once, Blanche loved Harry once, but things are different now. And as the heart lands somewhere, anywhere, Harry and Dr Cobbett come in at the gate. And from the verandah Cissie is waving and: Dear old girl, thinks Harry as he sees her, dear old wifey. For Cissie isn't much to look at, but Harry has had a bad scare; this time the feeling of guilt was so keen that he hardly though he'd survive it. This time, as well as worrying over what he'd done with Blanche, he'd worried that Tempe would betray him. But worrying has served its purpose, for now it's a quiet life for Harry Jones; now Harry will beg pardon of God, and go on to play the part of hubby with gusto. He will make himself more married than ever; it will mean an extra barrier between Harry and memory, between Harry and Tempe, between Harry and Blanche: God willing, Harry will grit his teeth hard and give Cissie a child; God willing, also, that feeling of peace he knew on the gum-field will one day be Harry's again (surely, with Cissie as millstone round his neck for life, he'll deserve it?). And on the verandah Cissie waves on, and now that the men are closer Cissie is calling out. "Tempe is gone," she calls. Tempe has fled into the forest, Cissie thinks. And so Harry and Dr Cobbett run under the pine-trees, too.

The forest was full of shadows; sometimes Ida ceased feeling excited to be afraid. Pines were such inky-blue trees; the wind whispered through them. Pine-cones were the skulls of dead babies; dead birds were everywhere.

Ahead of Ida ran Oc, she could see his Norfolk jacket and knickerbockers through the trees. Oc, in his pursuit of Augustus, had led Ida to the heart of the needle-wood. Massive trees were all about her; their roots and the lower portions of their trunks were covered with moss. High above Ida's head their branches laced in a network of foliage, which threw fantastic light and shade on the decayed leaf-mould and discarded needles beneath them.

Ida followed Oc, for she had a suspicion that he was trailing Maud. Maud was somewhere ahead and Ida was determined to save her. But then she heard a strange rustle; then she saw a strange shape. Ida could never resist a mystery, so she stopped following Norfolk jacket and knickers to move closer to the shape that soon stopped being strange, as it revealed itself to be the body of Tempe's runaway camel-boy. The camel-boy was creeping through the trees and Ida crept, too, and Ed Thrush led her to a coppice where the forest growth was scanty, except in one spot that partly enclosed a pool. It was a smaller pool than the one that Tempe occasionally floated in; it was situated in a little hollow, a mere dip or depression. Ida watched Ed sink down behind a bush that grew beside it.

Trees bearing berries were reflected in the water, as in a mirror. It was cool, for there is moisture in a needle-wood in even the hottest weather. Ida held her breath and watched the crouching camel-boy and wondered what it was that he awaited. Then a sound like a stick being snapped in two reached her ears — and it was the clap of the powerful pinions of a wood-pigeon as he dashed from the tree-tops to drink. His mate joined him. *Coo-coo-cooee* called the pigeons, bending their beautiful necks.

And those trees round the pool are miro-trees, and pigeons grow fat on their berries (kowhai leaves make pigeons thin). Tempe told Ed these things when she invited him to the forest to live. "You will manage," she said. "I will bring you food; you must learn to catch birds." And she showed him how you set a snare by the edge of a pool where a pigeon, thirsty after eating miro berries, came to drink; how a slip noose on the end of a pole was used to catch owls and parakeets; how you could kill birds by striking with a heavy stick. Somehow Tempe knew all these things. When she called Ed "Tane" she expected him to know them, too. But when he was allowed to be himself — when he was merely Ed Thrush — Tempe was willing to show him, though she grew impatient when he shuddered as he held the first limp body in his hands. It was Tempe who plucked the bird's feathers, Tempe who cleaned out its innards . . . But she only did it once, they only ate cooked pigeon once. Ed didn't learn quickly. He knew how to kill a bird, that part was easy; he liked to kill (when he killed he felt like a god), but when the bird's body lay in his hands he felt sick — dead bird wasn't something that he could stomach. He was a town boy; he wanted Ma Thrush and Queen Street and the tatty razzle-dazzle of the circus. He was tired of wearing a loin-cloth and a necklace; of killing birds and then feeling queasy.

But he kept trying. As the pigeons *coo-cooeed*, Ed crept closer, and by the edge of the pool was a snare made of cabbage-tree leaves, which Ida hadn't noticed before. One of the pigeons had settled in it, and Ed pulled a cord, and the bird's legs were caught in a noose. The bird fluttered wildly. Ed killed it by crushing its head with his teeth.

Ida hated him then. She hated the forest; she wanted dear blundering Oc. Octavius would never kill a bird like that. But where was he? Where was Maud?

Mr Maufe knew, he trailed her nicely. It was too easy, almost. To begin with, he'd proceeded with caution, careful not to let twig or leaf betray his presence. But she never looked round; but she didn't look back. In the end he pursued her with mock-nonchalance. Whistling, he tilted his top hat to the back of his head; he struck a path through the undergrowth with his walking-stick.

He would get her, he knew. She would stay with him for life. His love-charged hands would furl tight about her — they'd still be round her when the earth tilted to meet her. He'd love her even better then, down on the moist forest floor. Dear Master Bob. Who cared what the consequences of that ultimate loving confrontation would be? — not Augustus Maufe, treading the forest in silk hat and spats and the sort of frock-coat that vested its wearer with a certain aspect of dignified import, a sure moral and social superiority.

Decently attired, Augustus breathed fast, his whistling lost tune. Her silky hair stirred rhythmically on her back, it rippled provokingly. Augustus would stroke her hair soon, he'd wind it round his fingers as Young Apollo, once, had wound a skein of wool for Mama. He'd spread her hair over her shoulders in a silken shawl; wind it comforter-fashion round her throat. But he'd hold her so gently, for Master Bob was precious. "Pretty little love," he'd croon. And then he couldn't wait — then his hands stretched out. Now Young Apollo is in his arms.

And he was mushroom-soft, he was dressed all in white; he was dressed like a girl till he was five. He had a fat pet lamb and Mama won the prize for her zinnia in the Flower Show and they did ring-o'-rosy round the golden calf, the animals went into the Ark, Moses lay amongst the bulrushes and you were so pure, so soft, the sanctuary's linen was ice-white. And Mr Maufe loved Maud, but she wouldn't love him back. She stood stiff in his arms, she froze his love. She was made of marble, of wax, of wedding-cake. And then he began to hate her, and then she began to struggle . . .

The hate is stronger than Augustus, now; it has escaped him, he can't chase it in Maud's direction. Hate has turned traitor and entered Augustus's head; a giant poppy flower-petals open in Augustus's brain and its fiery petals dip in his eyes. It feels as if he is bleeding, his eyes swim in blood and there are fire-crackers sparking in his head. His head is exploding and the red poppy is all little pieces, now; its petals shred confetti-dot small and his head will burst and he calls out. He doesn't feel Oc's hands round his throat, or feel Maud fight free of his grasp. It is a stroke, but Augustus doesn't know it.

He falls at Oc's feet. The giant tumbles, the robber-bridegroom is given up to justice, the greedy monarch loses his kingdom. Oc's papa is no one to be afraid of now. He falls like a stone; he will live like a stone — dead but alive — for the little bit of time that is left him. Mr Maufe will enter the box-room at The Peach Groves, and Mrs Maufe will come out. Zillah will abandon her visionary pen and re-enter life with all her old Boiled Bull-dog zest. Augustus's living-death will pay the forfeit that sets her free of an over-zealous spirit guide. Zillah will smile and leave off her eye-shade and embrace life as Oc's mama. Oc will smile, too, and stop thumbing as he comes into his inheritance at last. First thing he'll do will be to burn all the old King's books, the bonfire will be a beauty. And Queenie will run away with the man who has mirrors on his toe-caps and Ethel will give up Poesy to devote herself to Papa. For Papa took a stroll in the forest that led him on to a stroke, and so many lives were unexpectedly improved, Oc and Zillah's most of all. It will be cosy being King and Queen together. Oc will have no need, now, of Rose-bud behind her hedge of thorns or Snow-drop in her coffin of glass. For Oc will have Old Ugly . . . life will be perfect with Augustus taken from it. For there is nothing that Dr Cobbett can do. It is a jerky ride out of the forest for Mr Maufe. Wouldn't he die of shame if he knew that his frock-coat is dirty and his top hat has been left behind?

Maud accompanied them to the house. Her hair was still silken smooth; her dress was mostly un-crushed. Already she had forgotten that brief con-clusive struggle. She was almost herself — Maud Dean of Glenelg, but not quite. Tempe's drugging still had its effect (Maud has cause to be thankful to Tempe as her memory lets her down), for Maud didn't remember a thing . . . Not a thing since the fancy ball — since Mama bent over her bed in her frost maiden guise and kissed Maud to sleep.

It is strange to find yourself in a forest, and not know how you got there or why you should be there, but Maud doesn't feel worried. She feels strangely at peace. Though sorry for the old man they carry. Poor Mr Maufe. His mottled face looks more jewelled than ever — his old dead face looks on fire. But his eyes are wet and blurred; his old man's hands are so white that he might be wearing white gloves.

Once Maud had courted those hands, sure that at their touch something wonderful would be revealed. But Maud was only a little girl when she thought like that; now, all unknowing, Maud has started to grow up. Her season as childish tempter is over, and something is irrevocably lost. But Maud doesn't indulge in any sentimental looking back. She never had much imagination.

And while they carried him to the house, Tempe

continued her search. She ran out of the pine-wood, out of the jungly part of the forest; she entered the overgrown garden and still she couldn't find him. She had searched for Tane everywhere, she had pleaded with Mother to help her, but Linda chose to keep mum. Tempe ran through the garden and felt terribly alone. She'd been so confident that she'd find him; so certain Mother would accompany her till she did. She must have done something wrong — but what? And it was as she wrinkled her brow and tried to solve the puzzle, that Mother's voice finally came to her clear. And then Tempe felt more abandoned than ever, for Mother spoke to her coldly. Linda's voice was unfriendly as it listed Tempe's misdeeds.

It had been a mistake to climb to the top of Mount Eden; for a mountain — even a tame one — should never be scaled, for mountains were sacred and the abode of the gods. And Tempe had killed the pigeon — that was wrong, too. And, even worse, once — remember — she'd looked at a lizard; once there'd been a lizard in Tempe's path, and a lizard was an evil omen, a harbinger of death . . . Tempe's offences are many; they don't bear thinking of. But Mother keeps telling them: Tempe stops up her ears.

When she unplugged them, the garden was quiet. The ivy and wild roses were still, each step she took made a loud noise. She came to the secret pool. She had floated on its surface, once, with daisies threading her hair. Mother had spoken kindly to Tempe as she played Lady. But not now.

For Tempe has waded into the pool; she has lain herself down to be cradled by star-grass and milfoil.

The willows lean over her. Through their branches the sky comes close. Tempe concentrates on its uncaring blueness, and doesn't hear Ed Thrush push his way through the trees. But she isn't surprised when he blocks out the sky. He stands over her with the willows making shadow patterns on his body.

Ed Thrush seized Tempe's body. He wrapped his arms round her; he looked pleased to find her, Ida thought. They stood close, it was as if they embraced: Ida was glad she had followed Ed to the pool, for his reunion with Tempe was romantic. But then Tempe pushed him away; then she fought him and her voice was ugly. Ida couldn't understand the words — only when she called out for Tane. Tempe spoke a foreign language, but Ed's hands kept holding her. The star-grass wobbled. They grappled together; their bodies were wet. Then Ed clasped her harder, he loved her more.

Somehow it happened. Tempe fell back into the water and the pool took her. It was hard to see what happened. She sort of twisted when Ed put out his hands to save her.

Is he drowning her, or does she push him away and embrace the water herself? Ida doesn't know, she will always wonder.

Tempe floated face down in the pool and Ed Thrush climbed out. He ran back into the forest. With luck he would find his way to Auckland.

5

"My dear old Georgie,

A mail leaves for Sydney today so you will get this, I hope, a few days before departing for Melbourne. We leave Epsom on Friday and I can't tell you how glad I am that the day is so near. I am longing to be with you, and I wouldn't stay another month with Cissie and Harry if anyone gave me a hundred pounds to do so . . ."

God was good. Blanche had George: she could write him a letter. All was for the best. George might be stout and a bore, but he was also rich and classy and kind. And home meant Dandie and Dash and as much fruit as you cared to eat and the window open in the drawing-room and no lunatic half-sister drowning herself in a pool . . . and there was a cave, as well, lined with sea-shells and in it, on a stone table with legs fashioned like dolphins, were numerous bottles. And: "Poison," Dr Cobbett reckoned, wrinkling his nose and: "She tried to poison me," said Cissie and: Me, too, thought

Blanche. But she didn't say it, for she was Blanche Dean of Glenelg, South Australia and things were arranged differently at home.

Adelaide was the City of Churches, and nothing bad happened to a Dean. Not a hint of scandal should reach George's ear. A Dean wasn't related, however tenuously, to a loony; a Dean was nothing to do with that previous figure they'd carried in from the forest (even though *he* was related to Lord Fermoy). Oh, but it was tiresome that such a nice old man should, without warning, turn so unknowable. He was so perfectly repulsive lying there, so dead yet alive, that Blanche couldn't bear to look. There was no point in knowing Augustus Maufe, now. What a pity he hadn't the forethought to introduce Maud to Remenyi before taking his stroke.

George must never know. Blanche had spoken to the little girls and they'd promised faithfully to keep silent. Maud wouldn't mention Mr Maufe's mishap; Ida would keep quiet about Tempe. For it had been Ida who'd found the body, floating. A nasty experience for a child, you'd think — but Ida took it calmly. A strange child, Ida ... a Dean through and through. Nothing made much impression on Ida. Certainly not Tempe Wimperis's death.

Not to worry, though, for they were going home and George had sent another ten pounds, which meant that Blanche had sufficient spon in hand to account for their final expenses nicely ... There was their washing, of course, and new shoes and gloves for the girls. Then Blanche must buy two pairs of terra-cotta plaques to give Cissie before they departed. Maud was going to paint one pair and Blanche the other, and then they'd be mounted in plush. Then, too, Blanche and the girls must have their likenesses taken, as there was a splendid photographer in Auckland ... and perhaps some good views of the town to bring home ... and then, with two or three little donations ... Really, the money just melted away. And Cissie had borrowed ten shillings from Blanche the first week they were there, and had quite forgotten it. Blanche looked on it as ten shillings wasted.

But God was good, Blanche had money in her purse; all was for the best. Cissie might have to wear mourning for the sister she'd hated, but they were lunching at the Van der Heydens', and tomorrow was the Alexanders' tea-party. There was a pattern, and Blanche's letter to George would reflect it. Not Mr Maufe, not Tempe, but: ". . . cut out chemise for Cissie ... watered lily-bed, gardened ... read Rosa Nouchette Carey on balcony ... croquet at Lieutenant Colonel Mawson's — four games, I won them all . . ."

Quite a crowd came to see them off and say goodbye: Mr Van der Heyden and his two daughters, Mr and Mrs Hunt, the Alexanders, the Mawsons and Aunt Cissie and Uncle Harry, of course.

There was a gale blowing all round the coast when they left and they came in for it. They were not frightened, however, for the *Tarawera* was a grand ship and rolled far less than either the

Ringarooma or the *Valetta*. At Gisborne and Napier they did not go ashore, as they were lying out, far from land. It was frightfully rough at Napier.

They arrived in Wellington on a glorious day, bright but chilly, rather frosty. After lunch they went for a walk in the town and explored the Museum, where they saw a small collection of smoked Maori heads.

They were all very well. Ida had not been sick once; Maud, neither. Mama hadn't missed appearing to meals except dinner on Saturday and breakfast on Sunday.

Captain Sinclair was a silent old fellow, but Mama sat beside him at table and they had some quiet little jokes now and then. Mama reckoned that the *Tarawera* beat the P. & O. line easily — everything was done on a most liberal scale; there was no stinginess here.

They lay off shore at Christchurch and Dunedin, too, and the night they left the Bluff, the ship danced like a cockle-shell and the waves were like the end of the world. The gale was so bad that, just as the electric lights were all doused, one of the sails was blown to ribbons and the sea carried the third officer up from the main deck on to the poop. The engines stopped and they thought they had gone on a rock. That night Ida and Maud were afraid, and Mama sat up with them till three o'clock.

All next day it blew hard and they pitched and tossed terribly. The scenes at luncheon were ludicrous. The soup tureen turned over and fell to the floor; hot liquid was everywhere, and macaroni floated about like small eels. The children felt sick, but had good appetites, and Maud was well enough to sing at the passengers' concert.

Hobart was a disappointment. It was Apple Land and the home of the Tasmanian tiger, but they might have been anywhere . . . though there were fern fronds as well as chops in the butchers' windows and they saw Sir John Franklin's statue.

As they drew closer to Melbourne the sea grew calmer, and the evening before disembarking they watched a splendid sunset.

They stood on deck and gazed at the fiery sky, and Ida felt relieved. For they had made it, they were almost there. Soon they'd be with Papa, and they'd see the Yarra and the monkeys in Mr Cole's Book Arcade.

They gazed at the sky . . .

And Maud thought of new dresses, for Mama said she'd quite outgrown those she owned, and would be measured for several in Melbourne. And wasn't it nice to be a favourite on board, wasn't that new friend of Mama's charming? — and aristocratic, too, for he was a nephew of old Sir Robert Torrens. He'd promised to see them off with their luggage.

And Ida was happy, oh yes, for she'd seen the dreamland at last — it had been a perfect holiday, Uncle was lovely . . . But the first thing she'd do when they got home, would be to unpick that cross-stitch WORTHLESS from Queechy's stomach. For she didn't want any reminders — of New Zealand, of Uncle, of anything . . . But Queechy's glass eyes were knowing. They recalled Mr Maufe's sugar crystal moustache and Mama's night as Arctic Maiden; they told of Maud squirming on the grass and the camel-boy's last fearful grappling with Tempe; they made you hear Zillah's *Take care* and Tempe's crazy song as she floated in the pool. In any case, Ida was too old, now, to play with a doll (though Ida will always remember, though part of her will always be afraid, Ida is also strong: for Mama had never been a saint, Mama can never hurt her again: there are worse things than freckles, etcetera, which means that though Ida will hold Papa's hand in Melbourne she will really walk free — New Zealand had power to do that) . . . The waves were Ida's friends. They didn't betray her as she edged away from Mama and Maud, still gazing skyward as the orb of day sank in an amber glory (the poetic words are Mama's), to drop Queechy overboard.

And Blanche couldn't help it — she couldn't stop thinking; and, to steady herself, to stop the guilt that almost resembled fear, she started talking silently to George. It was like writing him the last letter of all:

Do you know, dear old boy, that the day we'll meet you in Melbourne, if all's well, will be Good Friday? And fifteen years ago we were married on Easter Saturday, and one of us, at any rate, has never regretted it . . . Oh, but I am thankful, old love, to be here safe and well. That New Zealand coast is a dangerous one. The currents are always changing, the mountains rise sheer from the sea . . .